1

OGHI SLOWLY OPENED HIS EYES. The light was blinding. Something flashed at the center of a grayish haze. He closed his eyes, opened them again. The difficulty of this reassured him. This meant he was alive. The physical burden of struggling to open his eyes, of squinting against the light, was proof.

A ceiling tiled with plasterboard and lined with fluorescent bulbs appeared. Every single light was on, which meant it had to be a hospital. Only a hospital would require so much illumination.

He tried turning his head but it was difficult. The best he could do was move his eyes from side to side.

"Oghi?"

He heard a voice. A woman's. At first he couldn't make out anyone, then gradually a white tunic came into view. The woman, he assumed she was a nurse, walked right up to him. He could smell her. It wasn't a nice smell. Sharp. Like she'd just finished eating. What time was it?

Oghi wanted to say something. He didn't have to ask where he was, he already knew. Where else could he be but a hospital? He clearly wasn't on the verge of death. Not if he could smell her.

"Are you awake?"

The nurse leaned in close to examine Oghi's face and pressed the pager button on the wall.

"The doctor will be with you shortly. Do you know where you are?"

She looked at the clock and noted the time on Oghi's chart.

Oghi struggled to part his dry lips. No sound came out, only a little air.

"You're in a hospital. You've been asleep a long time." The nurse's voice was loud. "I'll check your blood pressure while we wait for the doctor. He'll have to examine you when he gets here."

The nurse took out a gray blood pressure cuff. Oghi stared at his arm held aloft in the nurse's grip as the cuff encircled his bicep. Strange. He couldn't feel the cuff fill with air and tighten. Nor could he feel it deflate. It was the same when the nurse unwrapped the cuff and set his arm back down on the bed.

The nurse jotted something on the chart and smiled at Oghi to show that she was done.

What about my wife? Oghi asked.

No sound came out. His jaw did not move, his vocal cords did not vibrate. Flustered, Oghi rolled his tongue inside his mouth and carefully swallowed his saliva.

The nurse said she would be back and left the room. Oghi struggled to move his jaw. It wouldn't budge. If he strained, his dry lips parted slightly. This time he tried saying *ah*. He heard a faint whisper as the air that had languished deep inside his lungs escaped from between his lips. That was it. No matter how hard he tried to form a sound, what reached his ears was not his voice. All he heard was a steady mechanical beat coming from the equipment connected to his body, and from outside in the hallway, courteously hushed sounds, the gentle squeaking of nurses' shoes.

After a while the nurse entered with the doctor. Though he'd never seen him, the doctor seemed to know Oghi. The doctor beamed and spread his arms exaggeratedly wide.

"Oghi, so good to see you! How long has it been?" he asked.

Oghi was wondering the same thing. How long *had* it been? How long had he been gone?

"Do you know where you are?"

Oghi stared at the doctor.

"You're in a hospital, aren't you?"

Oghi tried to nod. A pointless effort.

"Now then, blink once for yes."

Oghi did as he was told. He closed his eyes once and opened them.

"Good, that was very good."

The doctor's voice sounded strained. Like he was talking with his fists clenched. Oghi had never received such a rousing cheer before just for blinking.

My wife?

Oghi tried again to speak. The doctor lifted his right eyelid, then his left. Then he seemed to be pressing and touching different parts of Oghi's body. Oghi couldn't feel any of it. The doctor checked the numbers on the machines behind the bed, wrote things down on his chart, and whispered instructions to the nurse.

"Good job, Oghi! You've done splendidly, and now you'll have to be strong again. Understand? The real fight starts now. Your willpower is the most important thing from here on in. That's what you need: willpower, not medical power. I'm going to have my hands full trying to help you get better. I'll do my absolute best. But my task is nothing compared to yours. Understand? It's not me, the doctor, who has to fight now, it's you. But first, we need to run a few tests, so we're moving you to another room. Okay? Blink once to show you understand."

Oghi again did as he was told.

"Excellent! Good job. Very, very good. I'll see you again in a moment."

With that last bit of exaggerated praise, the doctor left with the nurse.

The doctor had praised Oghi for regaining consciousness. A good job. Oghi chewed over the doctor's words.

Was his waking up really a good thing? The phrase the doctor had used—willpower, not medical power—nagged at him. Those words said a lot.

After a while, the nurse came back. She unplugged a number of cords that connected Oghi to the machines, then double-checked the bed and slowly wheeled him out into the hallway.

Oghi lay there and watched as the hospital ceiling and fluorescent lights rushed past. He had a feeling he would be in that bed for a while. Not just a few hours but for days to come. All this talk about the importance of willpower must have meant that, unless he wanted it badly enough, he would have a tough time getting better. It meant there was absolutely no chance his body would mend on its own, that even repeated treatment would not guarantee recovery. The doctor's and nurse's reactions told Oghi that he'd taken a long time to wake up. He'd probably received all sorts of medical care already. The cables, the respirator, the tubes snaking in and out of him told him that his had not been an easy fight.

The bed rattled and glided along and then came to a stop. They were in front of an elevator. It looked like it was meant for transporting patients only, but perfectly healthy people kept crowding in after them. As each new person squeezed in, the nurse nudged Oghi's bed further to the side. The people on their feet stole glances at Oghi on his back.

It was only after he was on the elevator that Oghi realized he was back in the real world. Not the hospital room with its excessive illumination, the nurse gently examining him, the doctor patting him on the back and telling him "great job" when all he did was blink his eyes. What he'd really returned to was this noisy, crowded, queuing, waiting, leering world. The world where, as his doctor explained, the only way to survive was through sheer force of will.

Oghi had nothing to do during the examination. There was no need for him to lie down in the MRI scanner, no need to stick out his arm so they could collect his blood, no need to remove any medical sensors himself. Unable to feel a thing, Oghi was shuffled from one bed to another, had sensors attached to him and removed from him, blinked as the doctor instructed, but mostly he lay there with his eyes closed. When the examination was nearing its end, he drifted to sleep.

As his vision went dark, Oghi saw over and over the car carrying him and his wife crash into a tall concrete barricade. He was clearly imagining it. He knew this because he could see himself inside the crumpled vehicle. And yet his head ached badly. As if he had slammed his head against a wall or been struck with something dangerous and sharp.

Inside that hazy white light that he knew was there even with his eyes closed, Oghi thought about whether he was going to survive, and, if this was the shape he had to live in now, what he should do, and whether he wanted to live anyway.

He brooded over what the doctor had said. He floundered back and forth between the pessimism of "exercise willpower" and the optimism of "a little more." But he couldn't help seeing more meaning in the adverbial phrase than in the imperative. Didn't it mean he would be okay if he just put in a little more effort? If he tried harder, wouldn't he be able to move his jaw to speak and walk on his own two feet into the examination room? There was no doubt. Oghi was counting on the world of "a little more." He wanted so badly to live.

How much time had passed since the checkup? Several days? A few hours? He couldn't be sure. The inside of his head was fuzzy, as if he were still dreaming, but his eyes smarted from the light. He felt like they'd just been tested for glaucoma, the light squeezing his pupils was excruciating. Oghi blinked slowly to check that he could still will his eyelids to move. He was relieved to find that part of his brain still responded to his command.

The door made a soft sound as it opened. Someone crept into the room. Oghi watched. The person, who'd come over to the side of his bed now, was dressed in white, and as he watched, its body stretched out long and thin and went up to the ceiling. Oghi stared in fear at the person crouched on the ceiling tiles above him.

It descended slowly toward Oghi. He closed his eyes. He shut them tight. He was determined not to open them. That was the only way he could fight his fear. It couldn't be a hallucination. He'd definitely heard the door open. More than that, the person sticking its face close to Oghi's now gave off a familiar smell.

His wife's smell.

2

WOMEN HAD OFTEN SERVED AS turning points in Oghi's life.

That was certainly true of his mother. She'd died when Oghi was ten. Oghi thought at first that her death was caused by illness. She was frequently bedridden and took prescribed pills with every meal.

Oghi didn't realize he was mistaken until after he overheard his relatives whispering in the hospital corridor. His mother had swallowed too many pills at once, causing her organs irreparable damage.

He only got to see his mother one time in the hospital. He couldn't remember whether that was because his father didn't allow him to visit or because her stay was so short. Cables snaked between his mother's prone body and machines attached to the walls. Sustaining a life seemed to require a tremendous amount of assistance.

Oghi's mother gestured for him to come closer. He couldn't bear to take her hand. A hole had been cut beneath her larynx; a breathing tube inserted there led down into her lungs. He had never seen anything like it before. Instead of taking her hand, he probably burst into tears or froze in fright. He may not have understood exactly what it meant to take your own life, but ten years was still old enough to have a rough idea of it. Seeing his mother in such a terrible state filled him with pity and fear.

His mother's death was Oghi's exit out of childhood. His obtuse, indifferent father either didn't notice the change in him or pretended not to. Oghi stopped caring about anything. He no longer complained about having to eat foods he didn't like or whined about needing to buy a gift to take to a friend's birthday party. He did not stamp his feet at the grocery store because he wanted something. He did not stubbornly insist on reading comic books for hours on end or playing computer games all night. Every now and then his father tried to talk to him. Each time he did, Oghi was reminded of his mother. He saw the hole drilled beneath her larynx, he saw the breathing tube. He couldn't help but clam up.

Problems arose at school that Oghi had no control over. News spread that his mother had killed herself, and his classmates began bullying him viciously. At the time, he couldn't wrap his brain around why his mother's death should make him a target. Only after much time had passed did Oghi understand that the other children were probably just afraid.

Initially, they simply avoided him without making it obvious. But by turning reticent and failing to join the chattering, giggling crowd, Oghi made it easy for them to bully him.

One day, as Oghi was being shoved around and hit by each of the other kids in turn, he bit one of the boys hard on the leg in defense. Oghi lost a tooth, and the boy lost a chunk of flesh. Oghi's tooth was just a baby tooth, but the boy's leg was left with a permanent dent.

After that no one teased or messed with him anymore. They all whispered that Oghi was as crazy as his mother. To show them just how crazy he was, Oghi would smile mischievously at them and then switch to a cold glare.

If Oghi's mother escorted him out of childhood, then his wife led him into the world of adults.

As college graduation loomed, Oghi prepared to enter the job market. This was before the IMF financial crisis, when the schools were still flooded with help wanted ads from businesses. Oghi was eager to get married quickly. His wife said it was too soon. She wanted to go to grad school, and she wanted Oghi to do the same. Though he knew he would have to live hand-to-mouth doing part-time work while barely covering his tuition and living expenses, he applied to grad school anyway without much in the way of a plan. He, too, was looking for any excuse to postpone taking a dead-end office job. He'd sent job applications everywhere, but he wasn't hung up on actually getting hired, and if the grad school plan didn't pan out, he could just send his resume out again.

His wife had told him she wanted to be a journalist. She wanted to be a reporter like Oriana Fallachi and do amazing, groundbreaking interviews with famous people. She carried a photo of Fallachi around in her wallet. Not one of her as a war correspondent on a battlefield, nor one of her interviewing Kennedy or Deng Xiaoping. It was a photo of her sitting in front of a typewriter, staring blankly into space, dressed in a stiff Chanel suit and wearing a pearl necklace—a vanity shot, taken for *Vogue* or *Elle* magazine. Oghi had no idea if that ridiculous photo actually depicted the "journalistic spirit" his wife was always going on about, but he did know that it showed what kind of person his wife really wanted to become.

Back then Oghi looked lovingly on his wife's shallow vanity. She knew exactly what her goals were, and though she believed in them, she failed at nearly everything she set out to do. Yet she brushed off each failure, hardly any worse for the wear. Then quickly found herself a new role model and extoled their virtues ad nauseam. By doing so, she seemed to come to an understanding of the difference between longing and ambition. While poised to withdraw her opinions, her preferences, and her own will at a moment's notice, she drew a line between what she could let go of and what she would hold on to. Though this tendency made her appear fickle and directionless to others, Oghi found it attractive.

Oghi had a fear of people who prided themselves on following a single path through life, who pursued their goals relentlessly, turning a blind eye to everything but that goal until they achieved it. People like that were so replete with willpower that they readily scoffed at the weak-spined. They criticized those who relied on luck, and they refused to acknowledge even the most trivial of coincidences. They were excessively stubborn and self-righteous, oblivious to how pride could turn into violence, and constantly spoke down to others. They did not hide the fact that they thought they were better than everyone else, and they mocked the sense of loss—of having lost out, been passed over, fallen behind—felt by those who didn't agree with them. Every now and then, they would make a show of being open-minded and magnanimous, their attitude one of grand dispensation, but this came less from a love of humanity than from the fact that they didn't have to worry about money. Oghi knew the type well. His father was one.

His father was a self-made man who had worked his whole life at the shipyards, and he mocked Oghi for going to graduate school to study cartography. A real man wouldn't be caught dead teaching, he'd said. Oghi suppressed the urge to argue with him, to tell him he'd get his degree on his own without any help from his tightwad father. His father was convinced—afraid, in fact—that Oghi was constantly trying to fleece him of his money.

Whereas most men seemed to be looking for some kind of idealized mother figure in the women they courted, Oghi had no such interest. He had a lingering impression of his own mother as someone who could stand up to his father and talk back to him even while in the grip of dark, pessimistic thoughts. She was at her most magnificent then. When she mouthed off at him. When his father lost his temper and lashed out at her only to be left more frustrated and foolish-looking as she glibly replied, "Why so serious? I'm only playing." When she laughed right in his face as he fumed and huffed and puffed with anger.

No, his wife did not remind him of his mother. Nor was she her complete opposite. In some ways, she encompassed both of his parents' personalities. She looked insecure but was full of confidence. She was self-righteous but easygoing. He marveled at her contradictions. It seemed an impossible combination. Whenever he thought about his parents, he pictured them sitting alone and sad in their own separate frames. They existed independently, cut off from each other, and yet they coexisted naturally in his wife.

His wife was the reason he went to grad school, but she dropped out halfway through her master's program. She claimed that she preferred to acquire real-world work experience and got a job at one of the online newspapers that had recently been launched. But she quit after just six months. After that, she sent her resume everywhere she could, trying to find other work as a journalist, but no one would hire her. She had no choice but to take a job at a magazine that no one had heard of where she lasted barely a year, churning out twelve articles a month until quitting that, too. Over and over, she went through the motions, sending out her resume again, or using the money she'd saved from her last job to do a little traveling first, before eventually finding another job at an even smaller magazine than the last, where she churned out the same number of articles with nearly the same content. In the meantime, Oghi completed his master's and finished his PhD.

Three years before they married, Oghi's father passed away. He suffered for six months before dying. The night the pain began, Oghi's father had met with some business connections. They were men who had worked under him before he retired. Even after his retirement, Oghi's father had kept busy as a supplier for the parts production company he'd started. He had followed their advice to increase production, but the international financial crisis led to a series of market slumps, and his father ended up taking a big hit.

His former employees had met him over sushi to tell him the bad news. The stomach pain started late that night. Oghi's father said that when he tried to stand up straight, it felt like a metal wire threaded through his intestines was being pulled taut. He blamed it on the sushi. It had been absurdly expensive, and when he'd gone to pay the bill, his guts had tightened into a knot.

The housekeeper arrived in the morning to find Oghi's father collapsed on the floor. She called an ambulance. At the hospital they told him it was kidney stones and that they had to operate immediately. The doctor scheduled an emergency surgery, but they didn't figure out until after they'd cut him open that kidney stones were not the problem.

Oghi finished his lecture at a university in Pyeongtaek and rushed to the hospital in Ulsan. It was the middle of the night, but his father stubbornly insisted on going to a hospital in Seoul immediately. They bounced from hospital to hospital, being told by first one doctor that it was irritable bowel syndrome, then by another that it was just constipation, and on down through a laundry list of commonsense diagnoses.

After a while the pain returned, but this time his father went immediately to a big university hospital in Seoul. It was diagnosed as an intestinal obstruction and he was sent into the operating room. Oghi was teaching at his alma mater when his father texted him the name of the condition. At the thought that his father's intestinal walls were in danger of rupturing because he had a piece of shit stuck up his ass, Oghi couldn't help breaking into random laughter in the middle of his lecture.

What emerged from his father's large intestine was not a hardened lump of feces. It was a tumor the size of a golf ball. His father was relieved to know that it had been removed, and he even joked about it. He said with a chuckle that at his age it was either going to be cancer or

Alzheimer's, and since he now had cancer he didn't have to worry about Alzheimer's.

The doctor gave Oghi a convoluted explanation. Though the tumor had been removed, another could grow back in the same spot, and if that were to happen, the tumor could invade the muscle fiber and spread to the adipose tissue. Oghi had no idea what any of that meant, so the doctor added that by that stage the cancer would be untreatable. And before long, that was exactly what happened.

After his father, who had spent his whole life handling iron, was laid to rest in a hard wooden coffin made from hemlock, Oghi received several documents. It was not a will. Just as his father had warned him, some of the documents would bring Oghi money while others would require him to pay back money. After doing the math, he found that he was left with debt. His father had spent a tremendous amount of money getting his business off the ground. But the amount wasn't so terrible as to make Oghi resent his father for passing away and bequeathing him nothing but bills. In fact, he couldn't help but wonder whether his father, who had always kept his ledgers meticulously balanced, hadn't planned it that way from the start: it was nearly the exact same amount that his father used to say he'd spent on raising Oghi while insisting that Oghi pay it back to him.

The year they married, Oghi's wife landed a job at a sizable publishing house, only to rage about her new boss's unbridled sexual comments. She quit after eight months but not before compiling testimonies from other women at work who'd been sexually harassed by him and posting an open letter to the company intranet detailing her boss's indiscretions—her version of a letter of resignation. Around that same time, Oghi had just taken his new PhD advisor's suggestion to change his dissertation topic and cut back on teaching hours.

Oghi and his wife were more or less scraping by. They didn't dare dream of having insurance or setting aside savings. The future was an unpromisingly distant thing, and the present was a repetition of similar, humdrum events. But day-to-day life was peaceful. They entertained themselves by taking turns reading the same book and talking about it when they were both done. His wife landed a contract to write a nonfiction book for a leading publishing house and started commuting back and forth between their home and the Yeouido library to write. In the evenings when Oghi came home from a day of teaching, she tried out new dishes on him. Oghi ate every last bite that his wife cooked, not caring whether it tasted good or not. They washed the dinner dishes together and took their full, sluggish bodies for a walk around their unremarkable neighborhood every night before returning home and sleeping soundly.

In the end, his wife never published the book. She didn't even finish the manuscript. Oghi had looked over his wife's rough drafts at least six different times. The opening chapter kept changing. The most interesting was the third draft, but she seemed to take Oghi's feedback—that it seemed too much like fiction for nonfiction—a little too hard. She defended it at first, saying that was precisely her intent, but she didn't keep it up for long. As if in direct response to Oghi's feedback, the fourth draft was a faithful litany of facts. Oghi told her it was about as fun to read as a newspaper article. The fifth draft combined both styles, which resulted in an introduction that sounded more like the opening to a familiar and clichéd genre novel, while the sixth draft was altogether different and written in an interview format, which led Oghi to scold her for being so inefficient.

After that, she stopped showing Oghi any of her drafts. She missed the agreed-upon deadline with the publishers, and in the end she gave up on the project. The publishing house suggested that she write a different book instead, but his wife broke her contract by wiring the advance back to them along with the not inconsiderable breach of contract fee. By then, Oghi had completed his dissertation and, at the perfect age for entering the profession, landed a full-time position at his alma mater.

They soon moved. The place they chose together was located in a townhouse complex. The house had the biggest yard in the neighborhood but was somehow below market, perhaps because of the state the yard had been left in. Nevertheless, the price was still too high for Oghi, who had just started his new job.

In the yard were the unsightly remains of a large vegetable garden that, had it been looked after properly, would have produced a sizable harvest, but was now buried beneath dead leaves that had withered and yellowed on their stems. As the elderly lady of the house's dementia had progressed, the garden had fallen into disrepair, the vegetables left in the ground to rot. Oghi wasn't sure if it was the fault of the dying garden, but the house struck him as gloomy and bleak. He felt the same about the elderly landlord in his shabby clothes and his crone of a wife who stared at them through vacant, addled eyes.

Oghi didn't care for the house, but his wife clung to the fact that it was below market. The old man was eager to sell it off, as it would be too big for him to look after on his own once he sent his wife to a nursing home. Oghi's wife talked him into it. Even so, he wasn't easily persuaded. He looked at several other places with the realtor, without his wife's knowledge. There was a house he preferred. But the price was more than he dared. After seeing that house, the house his wife stubbornly insisted on grew on him. Oghi decided once more to take a chance on his wife's certainty.

The day they moved in, Oghi and his wife turned on all of the lights inside and outside the house. There were a lot of lights to be turned on. After flipping every switch, they set the motion-activated light over the front door to stay on continuously. In the yard were fourteen lanterns of varying sizes. They turned those on too. Their plan was to leave the lights burning all night. Oghi and his wife wanted to congratulate themselves on their bright future.

That night the lights burned as brightly as the lights in the hospital room where Oghi now lay. Their plan was to leave the bedroom lamp on as well, even if it meant tossing and turning in their sleep. But when Oghi awoke in the middle of the night, the lights had all been turned off.

When did all that light first start to fade?

3

How does a life get so turned around in an instant? How does it fall apart, vanish, dwindle to nothing? Had Oghi secretly been helping this life in its plot to do exactly that?

Ever since struggling to raise his eyelids, Oghi had been asking himself a question. Now and then he got the same question from others: What on earth happened? He got it from his friends, from the insurance company employees, from the police officer who wanted to close the case, from people visiting him in the hospital. His mother-in-law had not yet asked him anything, but their conversation would probably be the hardest of all.

Oghi hadn't been out of his coma long when he received a visit from a claims investigator at the insurance company. The investigator had already been to the hospital once while

Oghi was unconscious, and now that Oghi's condition had turned, he was back.

The claims investigator understood that Oghi was incapable of expressing himself with any sort of precision. The nerves and tendons in Oghi's jaw were damaged, leaving him unable to speak, and when he did manage to part his dry lips, the only sound he could produce was a faint whisper. Oghi's only means of communication was to blink his eyes for yes and no.

When asked, "Where were you going?" Oghi could not answer. He could only respond to "Were you going to Gangwon Province?"

Oghi and his wife had planned to take a short trip. She'd been shut up in the house for too long, while Oghi spent long hours away from home but wasn't able to relax when he was there. It was a peaceful trip, unlike the ones they'd gone on when they were dating. There was no need to rush around preparing food to take with them or to spend a lot of time hunting down some place that would be both cheap and clean. His wife had chosen the date and the destination. She had even squared away all of the reservations. Oghi was so busy with work that they were nearly unable to go and didn't leave until late in the evening.

When asked, "What was the weather like that day?" Oghi could not answer. He blinked once in response to, "Did it rain?"

"Oghi, were you driving?"

This time as well he blinked once and started to blink again, debating whether or not he should, but kept his eyes open after a brief hesitation. The investigator appeared to take that as a yes and wrote it down in his notebook. It wasn't a lie, nor was it the truth. His wife was driving when they left Seoul, but after a quick break at a rest stop, Oghi had taken over at the wheel.

Oghi would have liked to add that detail. It seemed very important to him. Because it was the sort of thing he would blame himself for and regret for a long time. If his wife had continued driving, if he had not been in the driver's seat himself, then the person lying in this bed right now answering questions, the person spending the rest of their life in the hospital paralyzed would not be Oghi, it would be her. He had no idea which scenario was better, but he was alive regardless. And he knew that, in order to stay alive, he had turned the steering wheel toward his side of the car at the decisive moment. Unconsciously. Just as any other driver would have done. To protect himself.

"It seems you accelerated suddenly. Do you know how fast you were going at the time of the accident?"

Oghi stared at the investigator. He might have rolled or circled his eyes. It was not a question he was physically capable of answering, and in order for him to provide an answer the investigator would have to rephrase it. But the investigator dropped the question instead.

"Did you see the car in front?"

Oghi blinked once. He'd seen it, but it was too late. If he could have talked, that's what he would have said. He was unable to brake in time. The rain had started sooner and fallen heavier than forecast. The road was slick and the braking distance short, and though he slammed his foot on the brake as hard as he could, the car had skidded helplessly forward. It was a common story, an everyday occurrence, and precisely what had happened to Oghi.

None of the investigator's questions technically required an answer from Oghi. All that was required was his signature for the insurance settlement. There were always more accidents on the freeway when it was late at night and raining, and in the event that the car smashed into a guardrail and rolled, the fatality rate jumped higher. Oghi and his wife were the victims of a run-of-the-mill traffic accident that raised no suspicions.

The investigator named a hotel and asked Oghi if that was where he and his wife had been planning to stay. Oghi tried not to blink. All he and the investigator had agreed to was that one blink meant yes and two meant no. He did not know how to indicate when he did not know, and so he simply rolled his eyes.

"No?"

Another question. This time as well Oghi kept his eyes open.

"Do you mean you don't remember?"

Oghi slowly blinked once. He was familiar with the name of the hotel. Of course he was. He'd gone there three years earlier for an academic conference. Then he'd gone back twice more after that. But it caught him off guard to learn that his wife had chosen that hotel. She hadn't told him the name, and he couldn't remember whether he'd asked.

If he could talk, would he have been able to fully explain? He remembered some things clearly. But there was so much more that he couldn't remember. The doctor had already given Oghi the clinical explanation for his memory lapses. He'd said it was very common to experience temporary memory loss or mental derangement whenever there'd been a severe impact to the brain.

Oghi remembered the moment when the car hit the guardrail and tumbled down the dark slope. He'd never before experienced that much speed and that much terror—it was impossible now to forget. He sensed that in the future, whenever faced with a crisis, he would retrace each and every move from that night. Oghi had been afraid, but since there was nothing he could do and no one who could help him, he did not scream. The close, sticky air had hemmed him in. He'd mistaken it at first for the texture of fear, but it wasn't. The airbag blocked out Oghi's vision and slammed into him. Overwhelmed by the unfamiliar pressure, Oghi, even in the midst of his terror, prayed for it all to come to a quick end.

He thought he would be floating when he finally came to. He thought it would be a textbook near-death experience—him looking down at himself with his face shoved into the airbag. But he saw nothing. Everything was dark and he smelled something burning and heard a faint groan. The sound was coming from him.

Where was his wife? He tried to reach for her but couldn't move. As if he'd been locked inside a small, dark, narrow box. The unpleasant sensation of claustrophobia and the anxiety of being separated from his wife filled him with despair. Perhaps the person who'd floated up out of their body and was looking down at everything was her. Sorrow overpowered fear, and Oghi lost consciousness again.

That day and everything related to it would come back to him little by little. As his memories returned, staggered and a little bit jumbled, he would piece together the events of that day into a convincing arrangement. It would happen naturally, with time. He'd suffered a temporary shock, and would remember everything eventually.

The sharper his memories grew and the clearer his situation, the sadder and more miserable and more heartbroken Oghi became. He found himself wishing for some memories to never return. Because the more he remembered, the more he would have to accept that he had lost his wife, and that he would never see her again.

The whole time that Oghi was fielding fruitless question and answer sessions with the claims investigator and others, his mother-in-law did not ask him a single thing. She simply stood in silence next to whoever was asking the questions. When she saw that he was growing tired, she asked them to stop or to continue later. When his interrogators left and it was just the two of them in the hospital room, she took Oghi's impassive hand and wept silently. Some of these moments lasted a long time, but she never so much as whimpered. If the doctor or a nurse came in, she just as quietly wiped her eyes and moved off to the side.

Each time Oghi watched his mother-in-law silently draw forth her sorrow, Oghi wanted to cry with her. If he could have moved his jaw or made a sound, he would have. He regretted not being able to tell her how sad he was. He wanted to apologize for the fact that her daughter died while he survived. He was sorry that they couldn't talk about his wife together. He felt an ache in his chest. It churned there and grew hot, and his throat closed up like he was going to vomit. It made Oghi think he was crying. He thought at first that there were tears on his face, but it turned out to be drool. Oghi's jaw moved a tiny bit, his dry lips cracked open, and instead of sadness, spit spilled out. Oghi kept drooling. He had no choice, as he could not yet close his parted mouth on his own.

As her tears fell, his mother-in-law patted his numb hand. He couldn't tell whether her hand was dry or damp from wiping her eyes. Every now and then when she took his hand, he felt something like a tiny jolt of electricity. He stared hard at her when that happened, but she was so lost in her own grief that she never noticed. He couldn't tell whether the jolt was a sign that he was regaining sensation, or just friction from the many cables connecting him to machines.

4

FOR THE OLD OGHI, THE word *disabled* had made him picture a veteran of some long-ago war coming home minus
an arm or a leg. It denoted the tragedy produced by a ques-
tionable mix of chromosomes at the time of conception or
by some bruised genes passed down through the family.
None of which applied to him. That word and Oghi lived
in completely different worlds.

Each time he was transported, prone in his bed, to the
examination room or the treatment room, other people
stared openly at him, or struggled not to stare. Adults usually made a conscious effort not to. They would examine
him when they thought he wasn't looking and then feign
indifference. Children were the opposite. They stared. They
tugged at their mother's hands and urged them to look too,
or made faces like they were scared, or actually said out loud
that they were scared. They trailed after Oghi and asked,

"How did that man get hurt?" or "What's wrong with his face?"

What Oghi hated even more than their innocence was their parents' pity. They pulled their children away by the hand and scolded them to watch their mouths. When they quietly whispered, "He had an accident, that poor man," he felt angry.

Some of them looked afraid. Couples grabbed each other's hands, people in conversation stopped mid-sentence. They paused whatever they were doing until his gurney had passed. Oghi wondered if they thought that by avoiding him, they would keep themselves safe from his fate. Of course, they could've had other reasons. They might have simply been reacting to the ugliness of his damaged face.

Even after several months in the hospital, Oghi struggled to accept that this was his body now. He found it hard to acknowledge that he would never again be in control of his own limbs. He did not know how to handle the disconnect between the old him and the new him. All he could do was foresee that nothing would be as it was, and he could not even begin to guess at how many things would be different in the future and how those things would change him.

He had to learn a whole new way of living than before. His meals were not brought to him as he sat in a restaurant. He did not get to savor dishes prepared with minimal artificial flavorings and assembled from organic ingredients selected not only for their nutritional value but for the flavor, ambience, and dignity that such food imparted. Instead he ingested uniform amounts of liquefied food through a rubber tube. He did not have to chew or move his jaw or work his tongue. The slippery mouthfeel and bland flavor of the formula was second only to the unpleasant sensation of having the tube inserted. Before, he'd been scrupulous about including probiotics in his diet regularly, and his intestines had worked smoothly, never relegating him to the suffering of constipation. That was all useless now. Having lost the ability to control his large intestine and sphincter, he was forced over and over to relive the grief of putting on a ghastly show for the nurse.

When would he get to wear the two suits he had bought during a trip to Italy with his wife to celebrate becoming a full professor? Now his choice of outfit came down to choosing which pair of hospital pajamas, printed with the name of the hospital and designed for easy opening and closing, smelled less strongly of antiseptic. Oghi spent his days prone in bed. The nurse propped his legs and ankles up on a pillow to keep his heels from touching the mattress. To prevent bedsores, she turned him on his side twice a day. Morning and evening, once to the left, once to the right. She groaned each time she turned him.

Even after waking from his coma, it was some time before Oghi saw his own face. It had been a long time since he'd studied himself in the mirror. Now and then he caught a glimpse of his reflection in glass. When he was moved to the examination room, he saw himself reflected in the walls or ceiling of the elevator. He spotted his reflection in the nurse's oversized wristwatch.

There were a number of things Oghi had never doubted in his forty-seven years, and his own face was one. After the lines and contours had settled into maturity, his face had only changed a tiny bit whenever he gained or lost weight. The elasticity and color of his youth vanished, and gravity had been gradually tugging at the flesh beneath his chin. He had acne and milia, and his skin was growing darker, along with other continual small changes. But even with those changes, his face had remained a constant. The bridge of his nose, not very high but not too flat either. The round-ish apples of his cheeks. The bushy eyebrows that needed a proper trimming whenever he went for a haircut. His eyes with their long, sharply creased lids. It was all gone. Now he saw patches of skin grafted on to protect the flesh under-neath, the prosthetic attached to his jaw to stabilize the muscles.

The person in the mirror was a stranger. The only thing confirming it was really him was the name tag at the foot of his bed. Oghi was more shocked than when he first learned he was paralyzed. He asked himself the same question he had when he first recovered consciousness—was waking up really a good thing?

He couldn't shake the urge to give up. His doctor's con-tinuous attempts at psychological therapy were not exactly filling him with hope. If he'd never woken from his coma, they could have given him a merciful death instead. It angered him that even that opportunity was lost. It was his wife's fault. The night he'd started to regain consciousness, she had stared down at him from the ceiling. She was the reason he woke.

At night, before sleeping, he prayed. For the world to end. For his symptoms to suddenly worsen. For him to have an adverse reaction to the medications. For his breathing to stop. Of course he knew, even as he prayed, that none of that would happen. The sun would rise the next day as it always did and wake Oghi from sleep. The world would coolly start its day without him in it. And Oghi would exhale the foul-smelling breath that had pooled in his mouth overnight and begin another day in his hospital bed.

His mother-in-law stopped by once a day to visit him. Each time, she fixed him with a look of deep concern and asked the nurse about his condition, and then asked Oghi as well, who was clearly not okay, if he was okay. Probably she didn't know what else to ask. After staring worriedly at him for a bit, she would do things she really didn't have to do, such as tuck his blanket around him or tidy the area around his bed. Then she would exchange a few more quiet words with the nurse and leave.

One day, she stayed longer than usual. Even after her brief conversation with the nurse, and even after straightening his sheets, she just sat there blankly on the chair beside his bed. Oghi gazed at her. She wasn't much company, but she was polite and always well put together. As he looked at her, he wondered if his wife would have looked the same at that age. When he pictured his wife as an old woman, he saw his mother-in-law's face.

The nurse stepped out of the room for a moment, and Oghi's mother-in-law got up and shuffled closer. She looked shier than usual. After a long hesitation, she took out a small velvet pouch. She stood there quietly, the pouch clutched tightly in her hand. People walked past outside the door just then, startling her, and she shoved it back into her bag. After a brief moment, she calmed herself and took it out again.

"Do you know what this is?" she asked.

It was a ring, with a diamond about five millimeters in diameter.

Oghi didn't blink. He knew it was a ring but he figured that wasn't what she was asking.

"My daughter was wearing it."

Oghi had no memory of his wife ever owning that ring.

"The police gave it to me."

She covered her face, the ring still clutched tightly in her hand. She looked like she'd started crying again. Oghi waited. She wasn't being untoward. Maybe she missed her daughter and wanted to talk about her, or maybe she just wanted to touch an object that reminded her of her daughter and talk about it.

The nurse opened the door but quietly closed it again when she saw that Oghi's mother-in-law was crying. It wasn't the first time. She cried easily, and pointlessly. But something was different this time.

"Can I keep it?" she asked through tears. "It's the only thing I have of hers."

Oghi hurriedly blinked once. It would've been better if he could have voiced his answer: *Of course, you must keep it, it's only natural that you do, it belongs with you.* He would have said the words over and over, to keep his mother-in-law from feeling embarrassed about proffering such an expensive ring, to say that of course she had a right to keep the ring.

"I'm sorry. It's not mine to take."

It's okay, of course you should keep it, was what he wanted to tell her. But unable to speak, all he could do was blink once.

"I can keep it?" she asked again shyly. She kept her eyes fixed on Oghi, as if she absolutely had to have his permission.

It's already yours, Oghi blinked. He moved the muscles of his wobbling jaw and tried to smile.

"Thank you. I knew I should ask first. It's not right to just take something, even if the owner has passed away. It's just not done. Especially not something so valuable. But this ring. . . I can't believe she's gone."

His mother-in-law squeezed Oghi's hand. She cried. Oghi wanted to squeeze her hand back. To keep his honest and sensible mother-in-law from feeling embarrassed. To let her know that if anyone should keep his wife's last effects, it was her.

His mother-in-law's quiet tears suddenly stopped. Her eyes widened and she stared at Oghi. He understood why, he'd felt it too. She hurriedly called in the nurse, who studied Oghi for a moment and then paged the doctor. After a few checks, the doctor informed Oghi that his left hand was recovering motor function.

So this was what it felt like to survive. Oghi sensed it fully now. It had been so long since he'd felt this alive. Like he could do anything. First, his brain had awakened. It had suffered a shock and was sluggish, but it was slowly recovering. Aside from opening and closing his eyes, his body had refused to bend to Oghi's will, but not anymore. He could move his left arm; the nerves had healed. Maybe, after having gone to the brink of death, he was slowly stumbling his way back toward life one step at a time.

For Oghi, who'd found little reassurance in his doctor's attempts at pep talk, his willpower was returning on its own. Thanks to his left arm, he became aware of what he still had, what made life worth clinging to. There were so many things. He felt like he could grasp all of those things with his left arm alone.

The mood in the hospital room lifted. His nurse started talking to him a little more. Though his mother-in-law had never been the demonstrative type, she cheered Oghi on by saying, "Keep it up! You've got to go home on your own two feet."

Oghi began physical therapy in earnest. A schedule was drawn up, and for several hours each day he worked on his rehabilitation. At one point he worked so hard that he burst a blood vessel in his thigh and had to take a break for two weeks. After all the effort, he felt confused and depressed and refused any further therapy.

"It happens to everyone," his doctor said with a shrug. "Whenever there's a physical injury, it's only natural to experience a period of chaos. The accident dulled your nerves and numbed you. So of course you would feel this way. You can't help but wonder, 'Why did this happen to me? How did I end up like this?' Who wouldn't wonder that? But it's also natural for you to keep hoping. Because you're a human being. First you get stable, then you throw yourself into therapy. But you don't get far. Because the harder you work at your rehabilitation the worse the pain gets. Meanwhile, recovery takes a long time, and when you realize it doesn't happen overnight, you get depressed and anxious. But that's okay. Because you're alive. Because you can do whatever you set your mind to."

The doctor explained in a kind voice that Oghi's case was not unusual and that it was simply what any person would experience.

Oghi was reassured. It comforted him to know that he was treading a path that many others had taken. He couldn't bear the idea that he was different now. That his being different was just another word for being disabled.

5

Two orderlies carried Oghi carefully through the iron gate on a stretcher. Oghi's prone position gave him an unusual angle on his house. Each time the stretcher dipped, the gabled roof seemed to warp and twist and cast out a long shadow. The dark exterior walls of the house pitched and swayed, and the camphor tree stretched its overgrown branches down toward Oghi's body. Then the porch loomed over and closed in on him.

It took a long time for Oghi to enter the room he would be staying in, the bedroom that he had once shared with his wife. The orderlies had not made a mistake nor had Oghi insisted on dragging his broken body into the room himself. He was in no shape to try. Despite three months of intensive physical therapy, there'd been little improvement. He was able to use his left arm and to turn his head slightly from side to side, but that was all. His left arm that had once filled him with the will to live now only made him despair at how little progress he'd made. Even after concerted effort, none of his other limbs had recovered. When he overused his left arm, he got cramps and the muscles ached afterward. The difference from his atrophied right arm was stark. Only the one arm had recovered, leaving his body out of balance.

What prevented Oghi and the two orderlies from entering the house was Oghi's mother-in-law. She clung to the side of the stretcher and wept. He'd never seen her cry like this before, wailing loudly like a child, her face twisted up in a terrible grimace. She'd cried frequently in the hospital but they were soundless tears. A mannered cry, quiet and cold. Even in her silences she'd seemed as if she were constantly crying. But in front of others, she tried to avoid revealing a single tear and behaved as if she had come to terms with her daughter's death.

It took forever for Oghi to be laid down in his own room. Instead of his Ethan Allen rosewood bed, the room held a low, narrow hospital bed, the kind that could be easily raised and lowered. The bed he had shared with his wife was too big and high now for Oghi. It was the only piece of furniture that had changed, and yet the room had the chilly, desolate look of a convalescent facility.

His mother-in-law had taken care of everything, from having him discharged to getting the house ready. She'd met with Oghi's doctor and scheduled his next operation, asked about his prognosis and told him everything that the doctor told her, made arrangements for an ambulance to pick him up for his regular checkups at the hospital, consulted with the physical therapists there about how his rehabilitation would proceed and hired one who made house calls to help with his muscles and joints. She had even purchased the hospital bed and all of his physical therapy equipment.

Other than his mother-in-law, he had no one else to do this for him. She was his only family and his legal guardian.

She had also hired his caregiver. She'd placed a help wanted ad online with the assistance of a nurse at the hospital. Since it was a live-in position, there weren't many applicants. She met each of them in turn and interviewed them, asking about their work experience and qualifications, and then selected one and negotiated the wages and working conditions.

She told Oghi that the caregiver she'd hired dressed like a country bumpkin, but what mattered was that she had plenty of experience.

"She said the last person she cared for was on the verge of death but she brought him back to life."

Oghi smiled. If he could have made any sound, he would have laughed out loud. His mother-in-law was not the type to exaggerate or make a big deal out of things. The caregiver must have talked herself up.

She told him something similar about the physical therapist who made house calls. That his current patient had made a full recovery.

"He said it took just one year for the patient to walk again. He must be very skilled."

If there was one thing Oghi hated, it was tales of miraculous recoveries. Back before his accident, he would have poked fun at her for it. He would have said that people will do and eat all sorts of stupid things just to survive. But this time Oghi wanted to chime in, to say he was paying attention. Because he could not, he blinked instead.

Oghi was still only capable of producing words that sounded like a moan or muttering things that no one could make out, but according to his doctor, his speech would get much better after his next surgery. The doctor said that the muscles of Oghi's shattered jaw were moving back into place, and his badly damaged vocal cords were likewise on the mend.

"Yes, yes, you don't have to thank me. I'm only doing what I must."

His mother-in-law responded as she saw fit. Oghi blinked, as if to say, sure, that was what he'd wanted to say.

"Who else would do all this for you?" She let out a low sigh and asked, "So, how does it feel to be home again?"

Oghi looked up at the familiar square ceiling lamp. It was so much dimmer than the glaring lights of the hospital room that he briefly wondered if one of the bulbs had gone out. It was cozy. The light made him feel safe.

"Does it feel good?" she pressed.

Oghi blinked hard. It did feel good. The past three months had been one miserable and depressing day after another. There would be many more of those days to come, but for now, he felt at ease. It didn't matter that his body was broken and he couldn't move and his wife was dead, he was simply relieved to the point of astonishment that he could feel this way.

"Of course it's good. It must feel good," she said with a sigh, and then suddenly sobbed.

He guessed she wasn't crying out of joy at his partial recovery. He figured she was crying because of her daughter. Crying with pity for the child who would never come home, whom she would've preferred to have home even if it meant she was in the same shape as Oghi. And because she missed the daughter she would never see again.

Oghi stared at his mother-in-law and blinked to comfort her. She wept loudly, louder than before, as if demanding that he agree with everything she said and praise her for her decisions. He was tired, but he wanted to do as she wished.

But as her weeping grew even louder and more ragged, Oghi turned his gaze to the ceiling. There were times when he liked the fact that he didn't have to talk, that all he had to do to communicate was blink and that, if need be, he didn't even have to do that. Now was one of those times. Oghi was exhausted. He was in no shape to comfort anyone. No one was worse off than he was. His mother-in-law should have known that. He'd been more than understanding so far each time she had looked at him and cried, but he sensed that it was going to make him angry in the future.

His mother-in-law's tears died down to a quiet sob. If she had let it all out at once, it would have tapered off soon enough, but now there was no telling how much longer her whimpering and sobbing would go on for. Oghi wasn't too happy about that. But then again, maybe happiness and comfort were now luxuries. His mother-in-law had been doing her best to bring that to his attention. Awakening him to the fact, as it were, that he had survived where his wife had not. Given the state he was in, Oghi should have envied his dead wife, but everyone around him kept saying how lucky he was to be alive.

Oghi wanted to be alone. He'd been away from the familiarity of home for so long. Even in the hospital, he was able to get some alone time. It was a two-person room, but he'd had it to himself whenever the patient in the other bed was in the examination room. It never lasted long. The nurse, the nursing assistant, occasionally his mother-in-law, or the family and friends of the patient in the other bed were always dropping by.

It felt more like being at a country market than a hospital. It was loud, and people were constantly barging in. Even when Oghi was emptying his bladder through his catheter, they would come in and try to talk to him, the door sitting open the whole time. He knew that since he would be relying on a caregiver for the time being, his desire to be left in silence was an impossible dream. But even so, as he looked around at his familiar home and smelled its familiar smells and ran his hand over his blanket and stared up at the pattern on the ceiling, all he wanted was to be alone.

His mother-in-law showed no intention of leaving. She sobbed quietly, and when the tears eventually stopped coming, she sat on a folding chair at the foot of the bed. She sat and stared at him. She did not take her eyes off him for one second, as if ready to jump up and fetch anything he might ask for. Now and then her mouth twitched and she mumbled something, but the words weren't directed at him. There was nothing he wanted to ask of her. In the future there would be plenty, but not yet.

He'd been away for eight whole months. He wondered if others had any idea what it meant to leave on a trip with your wife only to return home alone. He felt angry about the state he was in, and at the same time lonely at the thought that no one could possibly understand him.

Perhaps his mother-in-law would leave once he fell asleep. He closed his eyes. She didn't move. She kept her breathing quiet, as if for fear that even the tiniest sound would disturb him. He breathed louder. If she were watching closely enough, she might have noticed that his eyelids were trembling in an unnatural way, but he kept pretending to sleep. Just to be alone, however briefly.

It was the first time he'd been alone with his mother-in-law for this long. He'd been married for fifteen years, but they rarely had long conversations. There was never anything that he needed to discuss with her and nothing really to talk about. His mother-in-law was shy and not very talkative, while he was admittedly not the warmest person. Nor had there been any need for him to try to get closer to her. His wife had always been there as a go-between. His mother-in-law had sought her out and consulted with her in all matters, and in turn his wife was always the one to talk to her and only occasionally chose to involve him. When his wife wasn't around, there was his father-in-law, who was never at a loss for words. No matter the topic, his father-in-law always started out with name-calling and blaming others, but that didn't make what he had to say any shorter.

He remembered vividly the first time he'd met his mother-in-law. Oghi was nervous and had memorized his wife's two pieces of advice. The first was that her father was talkative and her mother was not. His plan was to be a good listener and applaud anything and everything his father-in-law said and to try to engage his mother-in-law in conversation. The second was, "My father has a lot, but I'm all my mother has." He took this to mean that her father was distant while her mother was clingy. His plan for that was to flatter her father for his accomplishments while praising his wife to her mother.

Oghi wanted to do his best and impress his wife's parents. He loved his wife, and he wanted them to be happy with the wedding. He was making a concerted effort because he knew he couldn't afford a fancy ceremony. Oghi was in the middle of a PhD program in the humanities with no clear future ahead of him, his parents were deceased, and he had inherited nothing from them. He was all too aware of his circumstances the day he went to meet his future in-laws.

His mother-in-law looked young for her age. She was elegant and aging gracefully. She had none of the dowdiness or pushiness that he normally associated with women her age. In contrast to his wife, who had sharp features and big eyes, his mother-in-law was plump and had a round face with half-moon-shaped eyes. But despite those differences, there was something very similar about the two of them. He hoped his wife would age as well as her mother had.

At the same time, there was nothing frivolous or casual about her at all, and that made him uncomfortable. If she'd been a little more down-to-earth, a little bit easier to get along with, Oghi wouldn't have had to sweat so hard all through dinner.

At first, the problem was his wife's father, who picked on every little thing. He seemed to know that Oghi was trying to get on his good side. But gradually, his mother-in-law with her unchangingly soft expression grew trickier. His wife was indifferent. She sat there as if she didn't even know them. It was strange. Of course it was only natural to feel awkward around future parents-in-law he was meeting for the first time, but even his future wife felt like a stranger to him. When he thought about it later, he figured she must have felt ill at ease too. It had to have felt strange to be sitting amicably between a father who was never home and a mother who had poured her whole life into her daughter rather than her husband or herself.

His mother-in-law chewed her food silently and stared back and forth at Oghi and his wife. The look on her face shifted very subtly from one of pride as she gazed at her daughter to one of doubt as she gazed at Oghi. But on the whole her polite, refined, and cultured smile never wavered. In a word, her expression conveyed distance.

Only his wife's father kept throwing questions at Oghi. They were mostly about Oghi's parents. No matter how he answered, his father-in-law punctuated his responses by lamenting over what a shame it was that Oghi's parents had died so early.

People were always careful when asking Oghi about his parents. That was how he knew that he had experienced something he shouldn't have at such a young age. They avoided talking about his parents as much as possible, and when the subject did come up, they made sincere-sounding apologies for poking at old wounds. This offended Oghi. It felt no different than when he'd been ostracized as a child. The message he received from everyone was that not having parents was a shortcoming. Everyone knew it, and they demanded that he feel inadequate for it.

His father-in-law asked him how his mother had died. What was wrong with her, how long was she sick, which specialist at which hospital treated her—he wanted all the gory details.

So Oghi lied. Since he'd been lying about his mother his whole life, it wasn't difficult. He'd been telling people that his mother died of liver failure, and in fact at times he thought maybe it wasn't far from the truth. His mother had suffered from depression and insomnia for a long time, and was doubly fatigued as a result. You didn't have to abuse alcohol or do hard labor for life to take its toll on your liver.

Oghi was flummoxed by his father-in-law's barrage of questions. He was acting like a specialist who blames the first doctor's initial diagnosis. The questions kept coming: How high was her liver index? How long did it take to reach that number? Wasn't the initial treatment mishandled? Didn't Oghi think to ask the doctor any of this?

It was worse when he asked about Oghi's father. Oghi's mistake was in mentioning the doctor who had diagnosed it as a bowel obstruction. His father-in-law called Oghi incompetent for not knowing any decent specialists and continued the interrogation.

He had no proper response to his father-in-law's criticism. He tried to keep up at first, but belatedly he realized it was only natural to not know the answers. As a result, he prattled on pointlessly about how they'd wandered from hospital to hospital, sounding like an idiot because of how little he knew, got picked on for that, and in the end found himself being asked, his father-in-law's voice laced with suspicion, whether cancer and liver disease ran in his family.

Even after they'd changed the subject, his father-in-law kept abruptly bringing up Oghi's parents. It didn't seem to be out of any concern that their deaths were caused by particular diseases or that those diseases might be passed down, thus inviting disaster into Oghi's future family. He simply seemed displeased with Oghi. As if it were his goal to remind Oghi that he had nothing. His father-in-law seemed intent on awakening him to his inferior position by telling him that he had nothing now and would never have anything in the future. Oghi's wife stared at the opposite wall, her face a blank. She made no move to help him. For all he knew, she might have heard it all from her parents already before they'd sat down together.

Finally his father-in-law jokingly asked Oghi, "Since you're an orphan, I guess that means you can skip the *pyebaek*?"

This was the traditional wedding custom in which the newly married couple bowed to the groom's parents. Oghi squirmed. His mother-in-law stepped in.

"Mr. Principal, I'm an orphan too. As are you. We all lose our parents eventually, so why are you giving him such a hard time about it?"

Looking embarrassed, his father-in-law reached for his water glass. He downed it in one shot and bellowed for a refill. Oghi scrambled up out of his chair, poked his head out of the door of the restaurant's private dining room, and asked the waitress to bring them more water.

His mother-in-law continued her quiet admonishment of his father-in-law. Oghi's wife seemed accustomed to her father's behavior and to her mother's way of nagging him and calling him Mr. Principal. A frown crossed her face but she didn't say a word.

His mother-in-law's words seemed to take effect, because his father-in-law did not say the word *orphan* again for the rest of the meal and stopped asking about his parents altogether. His talkative father-in-law swiftly changed the subject—right to Oghi's hopeless choice of academic discipline and his prospect-less future. Oghi was okay with that line of questioning. It had been an ongoing subject of conversation with his wife and cohorts and even with his PhD advisor. He and his cohorts joked about the amount of time and money they were investing in such pointless work. It helped them to shake off a little of the anxiety they felt about their uncertain futures.

Besides, looking like a deadbeat to parents was nothing new to him. Oghi's own father had considered him a constant disappointment. Every time he saw Oghi, he'd asked him, When are you going to start acting like a man, and, What kind of man sits on his ass all day fiddling with books? When his father said "acting like a man," what he'd really meant was "making his own money."

His mother-in-law laid into his father-in-law again.

"But Mr. Principal, you yourself taught ethics. You spent your whole life learning and teaching a useless subject. Who are you to criticize?"

She laughed as she said it, as if she were telling a hilarious joke. Oghi hesitated, unsure of how he ought to react. His father-in-law laughed. His wife, who had been silent and unresponsive, laughed a little. Oghi was the only one who didn't. The in-jokes they shared reminded him that he would always be an outsider among them.

From the appetizers to the final dessert course, his mother-in-law made flawless use of every bit of cutlery. Even the way she dabbed the corners of her lips with her napkin and lined her fork and knife up neatly to the right at the end of each course impressed him.

Oghi felt caught between his father-in-law, who used whichever fork and knife he pleased; his wife, who seemed to think she was above caring about such things; and his mother-in-law, who practiced perfect table etiquette. He kept stealing sidelong glances at his wife and mother-in-law before choosing a fork and trying to match the pace of his eating to hers. More than his father-in-law, who openly lambasted him, he wished to impress his mother-in-law, who elegantly concealed her true colors.

When the third course came out, she stared at Oghi. His father-in-law dug right in, followed by his wife.

As Oghi squirmed, his mother-in-law said, "Go ahead."

Her tone was kind and her expression friendly, but he felt he was being tested. She must have known that he'd been watching her the whole time. Or maybe he was imagining things. Maybe she just wasn't that hungry. Oghi was so nervous that he was seeing everything as a test.

Everything about that evening had weighed on him, from choosing the restaurant at Hotel Shilla for their first meeting and being told it was booked when he called to make a reservation, to then having his wife's parents call instead and immediately get one of the small private rooms, not to mention the smooth way his mother-in-law had ordered the restaurant's prix fixe meal for them in advance.

When they had finished eating and were leaving the room, his mother-in-law hung back. His father-in-law walked ahead, coughing and sniffing as he went. His mother-in-law looked back and forth at Oghi and his wife. Then she gestured at her retreating husband and whispered to Oghi, "You really hung in there." She added, "Mr. Principal likes to mess with people." Oghi waved off her concern and said he was fine.

"You're so well-behaved. If your parents could see you right now, they would be proud of you, I know it. I was a little worried you might have an inferiority complex because of being an orphan, but I see I had nothing to worry about."

She patted his hand twice as if to encourage him, said good night to her daughter, and walked away.

Oghi and his wife watched her parents' retreating figures as they quietly made their way out of the restaurant. After seeing her parents off in their black sedan, shiny from a recent wash and wax, Oghi waited for his wife to take his hand, but instead she raised hers to hail a cab that pulled up at just that moment.

It wasn't until much later that Oghi wondered if he should have been the one to take her hand first instead of waiting. He'd wanted her to comfort him, but maybe she was trying to figure out how to apologize. Then again, she hadn't offered him any apology at all. Not that he knew exactly what she was supposed to apologize for.

His mother-in-law's parting words kept echoing in his mind. "Well-behaved." "Inferiority complex." Those words dug at him more than the open criticism his father-in-law had unleashed on him all through dinner. He felt like she saw right through him. She knew that because Oghi had nothing, he had every reason to have an inferiority complex, and that he wasn't all that well-behaved either. His father-in-law had called him on it, and his mother-in-law in her own refined way made sure he didn't forget it.

His wife made no mention of what her parents had thought of him or what they'd said after the dinner. It made him uncomfortable to bring it up. He'd wanted to impress them but it didn't seem to go the way he'd hoped. For all he knew, she might have argued with them about marrying him.

After mulling it over for a few days, he finally asked. She shrugged. He'd been mistaken. He thought that she'd been avoiding the subject because they'd said bad things about him, but that wasn't the case. She simply had nothing to report. She told him that she hadn't had a chance to talk to her parents about Oghi at all. He was confused, so she reluctantly explained.

"They got in a fight."

"Because of me?"

"No, because Mom kept calling him Mr. Principal," she said with an embarrassed grin. "She calls him that whenever she's in a bad mood. She's making fun of him. He was never actually a principal. He never even reached retirement, let alone became principal. He had to resign early."

"Why?"

"There was an incident, and he took the blame."

"What kind of incident?"

"How would I know?"

"They're your parents, how do you not know?"

"Do you know everything about *your* parents?" she shot back.

Oghi tried to defuse the situation by laughing.

Only after they'd set the date for their wedding did Oghi learn why his father-in-law resigned. He'd been caught having an affair with a fellow teacher and was fired. His wife told him about it the second time he met her parents, about a year after their official introduction at the hotel restaurant. In trying to explain why her parents were so chilly toward each other, the subject had naturally come up.

Oghi went to their apartment, which they'd just moved into. It was in an older-style building, where the apartment doors faced out onto long outdoor corridors, in the Mapo district of Seoul. An oversized couch upholstered in water buffalo, the leather worn thin in places, sat in the living room. It made the long, narrow room even narrower. A flat-screen television hanging on the opposite wall was so big that it seemed to press right up against the couch. Oghi's father-in-law looked very much at home, sitting with both arms spread on the back of the couch and watching the golf channel with the volume turned all the way down. The people on the screen in their brightly colored clothes, tightening their buttocks and swinging their clubs, looked ridiculous, but the expression on his father-in-law's face was overly solemn.

His mother-in-law was wearing a housedress, the hem of which dragged on the floor. When she floated out in the dress to serve them tea on a shining silver tray, the effect was unsettling. The tea was scalding and must have been brewed from old leaves because it had no flavor whatsoever. Oghi blew on it to cool it down and drank every drop. Each time his mother-in-law walked back and forth through the cramped living room, her hem trailing, his father-in-law loudly clucked his tongue.

And yet for some reason, aside from the tongue cluck-ing, his father-in-law, who'd had so much to say before, kept his mouth shut this time. While his wife went into her room to change clothes, his mother-in-law pretended to read and did not look at Oghi or his father-in-law at all. Oghi had no idea where to rest his eyes so he slowly looked around at the interior of the apartment.

It was apparent that they'd come down in the world: the foreign electronics that didn't quite make sense there, the

Kim Ki-chang painting of a red bird that was probably a reproduction but still a rare piece, the designer shoe boxes that didn't all fit into the shoe cabinet and were stacked next to the front door instead. Adding to the impression was the fact that everything was too big for the apartment. The side-by-side Sub-Zero fridge stuck out into the living room, and small kitchen appliances—a toaster oven, a coffee machine, an electric kettle—were lined up on top of the heavy wooden dining table, making the living room feel even more cramped. He assumed the appliances had been placed there because it was the only space available; there wasn't enough room to consider anything like traffic flow while cooking.

Inside a glass display cabinet was a small lidded porcelain vase. Oghi stared at it for a long time. It was the only item that showed no marks of daily use in the cabinet, which was crammed with pots and pans, bowls and dishes, mugs and teacups, and other necessities.

Perhaps his father-in-law's unplanned early retirement and the need to reduce their lifestyle for whatever reason meant they'd had to sell off everything that was worth anything, and all that was left was that porcelain vase. Considering its unremarkable shape and its unusual blue tint, it couldn't have been very expensive and must have therefore survived the selling off of the family's possessions.

Oghi's wife came out to the living room and tapped him on the shoulder. Just then he realized that his mother-in-law was staring hard at him. His father-in-law likewise looked displeased.

"What a lovely *jagi* vase," Oghi said pointlessly, suddenly embarrassed.

His father-in-law clucked his tongue and slumped deeper into the sofa. His mother-in-law was speechless. The sound of children playing outside drifted in through the window, and she abruptly went out to the balcony and screeched at them, "Hey, hey, keep it down! Go play over there instead!"

His father-in-law clucked his tongue again and openly glared at her. Oghi was shocked. His father-in-law's odd demeanor and his mother-in-law's shrill yell had put him on edge.

His wife made up an excuse to get them out the door and led Oghi out of the apartment. In the elevator on the way down, she told him why her father had resigned. She seemed to think it was explanation enough for her parents' strange behavior. Before he could say anything in response, she burst into laughter.

"And the other thing, *jagi*, that's not *jagi*."

Oghi looked puzzled, which made her laugh even harder at her own pun on the words for "darling" and "porcelain."

"What's so lovely about that ugly thing, anyway? You have a terrible eye for *jagi*."

"Is it a fake?"

"Fake what? It's not a vase, I tell you. It's an urn."

"Why do they keep it at home?"

"It holds my grandmother's ashes."

Oghi tried not to act surprised. He was just being polite, but she seemed to find it more odd that he took the news so calmly.

"Did you know?"

"How could I?"

"The thing about my mom is, she's Japanese."

"Huh?"

"To be precise, she's half-Japanese. On her mother's side. My mother grew up in Japan until middle school, and when my grandparents divorced, she came to Korea with my grandfather. He remarried to a Korean, and since that meant she had a stepmother to look after her, there was no reason for her to return to her mother in Japan. Not that my grandfather would have allowed it. A few years ago, one of her Japanese relatives managed to track her down and brought that urn over. But can you guess why they decided to come to Korea after all these years?"

"To give her the urn," Oghi said, as if the answer were obvious.

"To go to Nami Island to see where that one TV show was shot. Because they're fans of the actor Bae Yong-jun. 'Yon-sama,' as they call him, was the only reason my mother was finally reunited with her mother."

They both had a good laugh over that.

"Why doesn't she have it placed in a mausoleum?"

"I think she meant to do so eventually, but it ended up staying in the house. She says the house she grew up in had a *butsudan*. You've seen one before, right? It's an ancestral shrine that's kept inside traditional Japanese homes. I guess since my mother grew up seeing urns in the *butsudan*, it doesn't seem strange to her."

"I saw one in a book once. It said the urns are only kept in the *butsudan* for forty-nine days."

"I wish she'd only kept it there for forty-nine days. . . I thought it was creepy at first. Whenever I pictured my grandmother's powdered bones in there, I couldn't look at it."

"What about now?"

"Now I don't even think about it. Every now and then someone will mistake it for a vase, like you did, and I'll have a good laugh about it. . . But I'm still afraid of it sometimes."

"Why? Do you hear voices coming from it or something?"

"My mother talks to it." She lowered her voice like she was telling him a secret. "She strokes it and mumbles under her breath. In this really babyish voice, like she's talking to her mother. That's when I feel creeped out."

"What does she say to it?"

"How would I know? It's all in Japanese."

"Wow, so she never lost the language?"

"Not all of it. She said her father didn't allow her to speak Japanese. That he got really angry whenever her mother spoke it. He was worried people would mistake her for Japanese. She told me that because she'd lived in Japan up until middle school, she spoke Korean with an accent and so she didn't talk much. I think she must've been teased by other kids or got funny looks from people."

It was the first time she'd told Oghi about her family. She might've not said anything before because she didn't think there was anything special about them, but to Oghi it was extremely interesting. He felt like he'd solved a riddle. It especially helped him to understand his mother-in-law. When he overlaid the image he had of Japanese people onto his mother-in-law, who was refined and elegant but difficult to get to know, certain things began to make sense. Though it wasn't a very nice method, whenever he felt like he didn't understand his wife's family, he simply told himself he was dealing with foreigners.

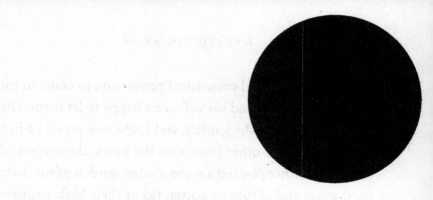

6

THE GARDEN WAS A WRECK. Oghi wondered how anything could fall apart so completely in just eight months. The plants stood, long-dead and withered, their roots still planted in the soil. The sight of those dead stalks standing straight and tall terrified him. It looked like the same garden he'd seen when the realtor first showed them the place. The same garden where the senile old woman and the feeble old man had watched Oghi and his wife from under the shade.

The garden that his wife had cared for was gone. He couldn't remember which flowers had bloomed there. That was partly the fault of Oghi's indifference, but also testimony to her design, so organic and harmonious that no single plant had outshone the others.

People walking past had often stopped to take a longer look at the garden after catching a glimpse over the low iron fence. Some had even asked permission to come in for a closer look. Oghi and his wife were happy to let them. His wife was proud of the garden, and Oghi was proud of her. Compared to the other houses on the block, the owners of which had either planted a more modest garden of similarly sized pines and shrubs or gotten rid of their high-maintenance gardens altogether and went for a modern look with only the house and bare yard, Oghi's was a sight to behold.

His wife had labored for years to bring the garden to that point. She'd failed the first year. She had planted a similar variety of shrub as the house next door, but they were all dead before two seasons had passed. The following year was not much better. The garden didn't begin to take shape until the third year. That was the year before last.

Oghi wasn't exactly sure why his wife had been so keen on gardening. But he knew when her enthusiasm for it had started. That is, when she started putting their yard to a different use.

They had originally used the yard for barbecuing. They'd furnished the yard with a large picnic table right in the middle, a sun umbrella, and two barbecue grills side by side, on which they grilled high-quality tenderloin and sirloin, sausages and potatoes, mushrooms and other fixings. Now and then they invited others and hosted cozy get-togethers. His wife's family and Oghi's old school friends came over. His colleagues also came.

It was after his old grad school friends came for a party that his wife changed the purpose of the yard. She sold the picnic table and shoved the barbecue grills and tools into the garage. Then she began overturning the soil. Though it was impossible to miss what she was doing, Oghi didn't realize just how determined she was until several days later.

Oghi was very busy at the time. He'd taken an interest in other work outside of his department that was worth adding to his resume, and was going all out with it. He put together a research team with funding from a foundation, was on several academic committees, and never turned down an opportunity to do consulting work. Books he'd published were being selected as recommended reads by different organizations and he even received the occasional lecture request. He accepted at first out of novelty, but later he kept accepting because he could reuse the same material. Some of his lectures took him as far away as Daegu, Gunsan, Busan.

Oghi had always had a hard time explaining what field he was in. Even when he said he did geography, people assumed he meant history. He'd taken pains in the beginning to explain that geography was the study of drawing the world whereas history was a form of literature in which you wrote about the world, but later he stopped feeling the need to explain. At any rate, experts knew the difference, and non-experts didn't care.

Now and then he'd get a comment from someone about how being a geographer must make him a whiz at real estate and that he must've bought some nice land for himself, and Oghi, no longer caught off guard by this sort of thing, would joke that that was why he'd bought a town-house.

He chose cartography for his dissertation topic because of his new advisor. The advisor, who was retired and busy writing his memoirs, had told Oghi it was pointless to spend his life studying topology in such a tiny country and urged him to switch to cartography instead. Oghi did as suggested. He felt compelled to follow this advice, since he'd been unable to complete his PhD before his former advisor had stepped down.

His former advisor got angry at Oghi. He warned him it was dangerous to specialize in cartography because the field had only recently gained acceptance in Korea. The only reputable cartographers were mostly from Europe or the US, which meant that unless you'd studied abroad, there wasn't much point. He gave Oghi some convincing advice: research on maps and mapmaking was still so new that the future of those scholars was harder to read than the maps they were trying to study. Oghi took it all to heart but did not change his dissertation.

His upper classmates gave him hell for it. They hadn't been like that at first. It started as reluctant praise. Gradually that changed to them saying Oghi was crafty. One said Oghi was the type who would abandon his wife and children to ensure his own success. They masked their disdain as self-criticism. Oghi had quite the sharp eye, they said, they should've been more like him. What was wrong with them, why were they so inflexible? Later they were open with their hostility: *Thought he was just bitching about his dissertation, who knew he was deliberately stalling for time? Son of a bitch was strategic.* Just you wait, they said, assholes like him always succeed.

In order to prove how wrong they were about him, Oghi poured himself into researching map projections and spent considerable time staring at old rectangular maps. He studied as many as he could, from ancient Babylonian to contemporary. The more he did so, the more forlorn he felt. No matter how hard you tried to draw the world, you could never be exact. That was what Oghi learned from his research. It was impossible to capture the trajectory of life in a map. Without one, there was no way of wrapping your brain around it all, and yet he was skeptical as to whether you could ever represent the world through maps alone.

But it was meaningful. Someone had taken these invisible trajectories that could not be studied with any sort of accuracy and had tried anyway to turn them into a tangible space. He found it boring sometimes for the same reason. A world that could not be understood perfectly, could not be explained unambiguously, and was interpreted differently based on political purposes and conveniences was no different from the world he was already living in. And yet, the one way in which maps were clearly better than life was that they improved with failure. Life itself was merely an accumulation of failures, and those failures never made life better.

Oghi wracked his brain for ways to put his studies to practical use. He noted the proliferation of mapping services like Google Earth and began researching the implications of online maps. This in turn led to writing a column and giving lectures. Ancient maps didn't profit Oghi at all, but when he combined them with Google Earth, it opened the door to opportunities outside of his department.

In his lectures, Oghi quoted the American geographer Waldo Tobler: "Everything is related to everything else, but near things are more related than distant things." But he departed from Tobler's original intent by using it as the setup to a punch line: "And that's why you better be nice to your kids and never cheat on your spouse." He closed his lectures with the cynical declaration that, "Maps do not show the world as it truly is. That would be impossible. There is no such thing as a perfect map and there never will be."

After his first lecture, Oghi was ashamed of himself for having prattled off a bunch of simple and obvious information in a voice obnoxious with certainty, but he soon realized that audiences found that sort of preachiness trustworthy.

When his colleagues regarded his focus on extra-departmental work and lecture circuits with displeasure, Oghi reminded himself that he was well into his late forties and fell back on his advancing age as an excuse.

Whenever he thought about being in his forties, the first thing that came to mind was his mother. Forty was the age at which she'd taken her own life. Forty was also the age at which his father solidified his position at work, began looking into opening up his own business, and stopped coming home at night. The forties were a turning point, as it were, the decade of your life in which you either learned to fit in or dropped out completely. Oghi, naturally, wanted to fit in.

To overcome his tendency to feel ashamed of himself, he took to recalling a poem by Heo Yeon that his wife had once read to him. The poem contained a line that read, *The forties are well suited to all manner of sin.* Thinking about that put him at relative ease. It reassured him to think that it wasn't just him, that it came with the decade.

Not long ago, Oghi had looked the poem up again. He'd been planning to write a column on the snobbishness of men in their forties, and he wanted to quote the first stanza. He pulled down every copy of Heo Yeon's poetry collections from his wife's bookshelf and studied the tables of content, but he couldn't find a single poem with the word *forty* or *forties* in the title.

He wasn't mistaken about who the poet was. He vividly remembered reading the poem with his wife and discussing it. They had talked about how the thirties were to Choi Seungja as the forties were to Heo Yeon. If Choi was the poet who gave voice to the cluelessness of one's thirties, then Heo Yeon was the one who captured the corrupt forties. Who speaks for the fifties? his wife had asked, but neither of them could come up with a poet and went back and forth suggesting different possibilities only to joke that the fifties were when you understood everything and so what was the point of poetry.

Oghi read through every collection of Heo Yeon's poetry and finally tracked down the poem. It made no mention of the forties at all, not in the body of the poem, and of course not in the title. His best guess was that they had assumed from the poet's own age that he was talking about that decade. Oghi was flummoxed. The first time he'd heard the poem, he was so certain that it was about one's forties.

As far as Oghi was concerned, there was no better definition than the phrase "well suited to all manner of sin." The forties were ripe for sin. And there were two basic reasons: either you had too much, or you didn't have enough. In other words, the forties were when you found it easy to do bad things out of power, out of anger, or out of feeling left behind. People with too much power got arrogant and easily committed evil deeds. Anger and the sense that life had passed you by messed with your self-esteem, made you feel low, took away your patience, and made it easy to package your acts as being about justice. If you abused power, you were a snob; if you lashed out in anger, you were a loser. Therefore, the forties were the decade that showed you what your life had amounted to thus far. Not only that, they were also the decade in which you could guess at what lay ahead. Would you remain a snob? Or be left a loser?

If those were the only two categories, then Oghi was closer to the first. Whether he was aware of it or not, he had gradually come to have more than others, and had blatantly resorted to underhanded means because he wanted to have even more, and felt no scruples about it. But there were also times when his life felt so perfect that he didn't wish to change a single thing. He did not want to lose a single possession. He was critical of his father's relentless drive for achievement, and yet he was already living by those same values.

Now and then Oghi would catch himself clenching his fists. Sometimes he wasn't even aware that he was doing it, even after they'd been clenched for so long that his palms had turned stiff and red. As he opened and closed his hands to release the tension, he would wonder just what it was he was holding on to so tightly. He never had to think on it long.

Though Oghi had never once thought of his wife as a failure, he worried that she might think of herself that way. Every goal she'd set out to accomplish had ended in failure, and she rarely got to feel what it was like to live up to her own abilities. It would have been better for her if she could have seen life as joyful despite that, but at some point she changed. She stopped seeing her friends. She stopped taking classes to learn new things, and she no longer mentioned any role models. She did not walk around with photos in her wallet or talk about wanting to write. She didn't even read as much as she used to, and would only flip through *Kinfolk* or gardening magazines from time to time. Sometimes Oghi would come into the living room and she would be looking around at their house and garden with a look in her eyes that said, *Where am I?* When he recalled that look, he started to wonder if she'd immersed herself in plants as a way of satisfying her hunger for life.

Of course, she could have had another reason entirely: to take the yard away from Oghi. Considering when she'd started gardening, that was the likeliest reason.

She had claimed the yard for herself after their last barbecue, when Oghi and his guests had stayed up late out in the yard, drinking and chatting and laughing and planning the next one.

Oghi and his guests had all gone to the same grad school, albeit at different times. M, who taught in the same department as Oghi, was the first of the group to graduate. K and Oghi finished the same year and interviewed for the same teaching position: Oghi got the job; K didn't. J graduated after them and started up the research team with Oghi. And S was Oghi's student and first teaching assistant.

There was a time when they had all felt the same uncertainty about their futures and harbored similar curiosities. Together they'd regretted choosing grad school, gracefully resigned themselves to their choices, and got drunk often. It was a time when their friendship had flourished for lack of hope. In fact, that was how they'd become friends in the first place. Then things changed. Their close-knit days waned, though Oghi still got along with them.

His wife had known them for a long time too. Whenever she joined them, she fit right in without any awkwardness. She was even the one who'd planned that night's party. She had sat at the large teak picnic table under the umbrella, conversing comfortably with everyone, helping Oghi to grill the meat, and quickly spiriting away empty dishes to refill them in the kitchen with something new.

Oghi had been very concerned, above all, to not look like they'd invited them there to show off. But in his eagerness to avoid doing that, he bragged instead about how big their bank loan was and how high their monthly interest payments were. He immediately regretted opening his mouth.

It was still early, but J got drunk and started nodding off. Since M and K's conversation showed no signs of tapering, Oghi helped J to the living room sofa before grabbing another bottle of wine from the kitchen. A few days earlier while at the department store, Oghi had found a very tannic French wine that M was fond of, and he'd bought several bottles.

No one else was drunk. Not his wife, and not any of their other guests. The hours had passed with quiet conversation over slow sips of wine about nothing in particular but plenty of laughter and no arguments. It was a satisfying get-together and a proper party.

His wife hadn't seen it that way. The next day she was indignant and lashed out at Oghi. He tried to appease her. To convince her that what she thought had happened absolutely had not.

This wasn't the first time something like this had happened. She had a habit of finding fault with some little thing and then blowing it all out of proportion and imagining the worst. She would become very sharp and high-strung and believe only what was in her own head, dead certain that she knew the truth. She'd reject everything Oghi tried to tell her and insist that he was lying, he had to be, as if intent on cornering him until he confessed. After she was done lashing out and venting her anger, she would eventually get around to apologizing. Then blaming it on her tendency to exaggerate and promising him again that she would try to think only positive thoughts from then on.

Oghi didn't mind so much. It was annoying, but he didn't get angry. After all, she wasn't *always* like that.

The very next day, she plowed up their yard. She wasn't satisfied with merely pulling up the dead roots and tilling the earth but instead seemed intent on turning over every last bit of soil that she set foot on. After she finished plowing, she went to a nursery, bought some seedlings, and planted them. They all died.

Then she got a little more serious. She bought gardening books, read them, spent the entire day outside, and consulted professional gardening manuals while drafting several maps of a garden. Each morning when Oghi left for work, his wife put on a sun hat with a wide brim that covered most of her face, regardless of whether the sun was out or not, pulled on a pair of rugged gardening gloves, wrapped a towel around her neck, slipped on black arm guards meant to protect her skin from UV rays, pulled on a pair of rubber boots, and went outside to tamp the soil flat. When he returned home in the evening, she was invariably sitting in the garden, still in the same getup but scruffier and more soiled than when he'd left. She only left the house to go to the nursery or to the Yangjae Flower Market. In addition to a trowel and hoe, she also bought a rake, a pick, pruning shears, wooden stakes, and burlap sacks, and explained the purpose of each item to Oghi.

Oghi suggested they hire a gardener instead. His wife was not so inclined. Oghi stood by and watched. Only when she announced that she was going to buy enough soil to cover the entire yard did he shake his head no and make his displeasure clear.

"We bought a house, not a flower garden."

"But we don't have any worms."

"Worms?"

"The soil here is dead. Who ever heard of soil without worms? It has to have worms. That's the only way anything will grow. Not only that, but the ground outside the house. . ."

She stopped there and laughed. Oghi had a feeling that what she was about to say next was not going to be funny, and he was right.

"It smells like ammonia. I think that old couple pissed in the yard."

Oghi frowned. If his wife was passionate about something, then he wanted to support her no matter what. He was fond of his wife who was gifted but failed at everything she set out to do, and who only grew more talented at sarcasm and derision without ever acquiring a sense of accomplishment. If Oghi had spent the last years expanding his domain, then his wife had been left further and further behind as time went on. When he thought about what she was like in her younger days, her current state was indeed unfortunate.

Nevertheless, the thought of her squatting in the yard and digging endlessly in the dirt so she could sniff someone else's piss or hunt for earthworms left him with a bad taste in his mouth. Of course he knew she was just trying to figure out whether or not the soil was healthy, but the bizarre look on her face when she told him the soil had no worms and the way she cackled as she pictured the old people pissing in the yard made the house—which he'd barely been able to afford—suddenly seem revolting.

His wife bought soil anyway and plowed the front yard again. She mixed the top and bottom layers of soil together to get the oxygen moving through them. Each shovelful of dirt was used to fill the space that had been dug before it.

To the right of their front door, she planted shrubs and berries, and to the left she planted flowers and herbs and other plants that required frequent tending. At the innermost part of the yard, she made a raised bed for vegetables. On both sides of the house, she planted trees. Right next to the front door went crape-myrtle, and to the right of the building she moved the two magnolias that were there when they bought the house and planted a camphor tree to the left.

To the right and left of the paving stones that extended from the front door to the front gate, she planted perennials: crocus, anemone, caladium, dahlia, ranunculus. Oghi called all of them *flowers* and could not tell them apart. His wife placed tiny placards beneath them. Sometimes she would cover one of the placards and ask Oghi to name the plant. Even though Oghi knew the right answer would have made her happy, he responded gruffly. She sounded genuinely puzzled as she asked, "How come you can't remember?" Each time Oghi inwardly retorted, *What's the point of remembering?* But the truth was that Oghi wasn't confident he could tell the difference between lily turf and lavender. Anemone and crocus were likewise hard to tell apart, as they were practically identical in size and color. Even when his wife explained to him that the crocuses had yellow stamens while the anemones' stamens were a darker purple than the leaves, it made no difference.

He especially hated it when she tried to tell him about the language of flowers. No matter what anyone claimed about the significance of flowers, they held no more meaning than the horoscopes printed in the daily paper. But she never tired of telling him about it. Things like, the language of anemones is fading desire or short-lived love. Though he nodded indifferently, he could not erase the thought that his wife was becoming insufferably immature.

The garden failed the first year. His wife was not as disappointed as he had expected her to be. She said it would take several years for the garden to flourish, and sat back down at her desk for hours on end amending her garden plan. At some point she said she was going to turn it into an English-style garden. What on earth was an English garden? Was it one of those gardens with all the flashy colors and irregular jumble of trees that somehow still made sense together? She started bringing him cups of imported British tea whenever he was in his study. On one of those occasions he caught a glimpse of her hands. They were covered in nicks and cuts from her gardening shears, and there was dirt under every fingernail. She said she couldn't feel the plants with gloves on, and so she worked barehanded as much as possible. When he pictured her washing and cooking rice and making soup from soybean paste and mallow leaves or boiling up a tofu stew with those hands, he lost his appetite.

Whenever he couldn't understand his wife's obsession with gardening, he thought back to how she used to carry a photo of Oriana Fallachi in her wallet and talked about wanting to become a journalist, and then he understood. Maybe her new goal was to be like Tasha Tudor. Maybe she wanted to write a gardening book of her own. Of course, like all of her other projects, that book would never get written. As far as he could tell, that was his wife's problem. Always wanting to be like someone else. And always giving up before she reached the end.

On weekends, Oghi had no choice but to help in the garden. His wife enjoyed setting him to different tasks. He quickly tired of scratching his forearms on stalks and stems and watching the skin swell and redden. He was forced to put up with his wife's scolding that he was deliberately doing a bad job in order to get out of helping her. But he actually enjoyed squatting side by side with her and exchanging pleasantries with neighbors who peeked over their fence as they walked past. He'd never exactly longed for that kind of domestic joy, but he couldn't deny that he'd pictured it now and then over the years. And of course, included in that cozy picture were geraniums on a windowsill, herbs planted in a large reddish-brown pot.

One day, Oghi asked his wife, "Why don't you hire a professional gardener and do something else with your time?"

She stared at him for a moment, her face unchanging, and quietly said, "Something else?"

"Something besides this, you know, something that will help you grow."

"I stopped growing a long time ago. Only plants keep growing, not people. We stop after a certain age."

"I don't mean that kind of growth. I mean find something that you want—"

"There is one thing that keeps growing," she said, cutting him off.

"What's that?"

"Cancer. Cancer grows in people even after they've stopped growing."

She giggled.

"I mean that you should find something you really want to do."

"This is what I really want to do."

Oghi realized he'd made a mistake. There was nothing stupider than telling someone to grow or to find themselves, but that's precisely what he'd just done. And to his wife, who knew better than anyone what a hack he was.

Oghi decided to leave his wife alone. It didn't matter to him what she did to the garden. No matter how much money she spent, he would consent to her wishes. She had the skills, and he had the means. His plan was to respect his wife's life, her preferences, her choices. In fact, he made that decision because he didn't want to care. But he did make one request. That she not cover the walls of the house with vines or other climbing plants.

Though he had no particular affection for plants, he did sometimes marvel at how trees grew so straight and tall against gravity. But he did not feel the same about climbing plants. They gave him the creeps, the way they would wrap around a fence or a pillar, growing in spirals, the stem circling and circling until it found something to climb, coiling itself around an object the moment the barest tip of the stem made the slightest contact, inching its way up. The stems were covered in suckers, and the idea that they generated enough suction to climb walls and fences and cover entire buildings frightened him. It looked dreadful when they clung to things, planting their roots wherever, willfully burrowing, gorging themselves.

His wife tried several times to teach Oghi. She explained that it wasn't strength or force that enabled plants to climb but rather a hormone within the plant that moved in the opposite direction of whatever part of it came in contact with another object. This kept the stem coiling inward and moving up and around the object the longer it grew. It was simply a different form of growth. He found her explanation convincing, but it still turned his stomach to imagine a plant with that much ferocity.

It was not long before the accident that Oghi discovered something creeping up the back wall of the house. He had no reason to be back there, but on that particular day, his phone rang while he was out in the garden, and he'd slunk behind the house to answer it.

Because he was in the middle of a call, he could not react as loudly as he would've liked to when he discovered the plants. Vines that looked like honeysuckle had encroached over nearly the entire back wall of the house. His wife had been growing them there, letting the vines grow thick and dense, where Oghi wouldn't notice them. It seemed she had erected supports some distance from the windows, and the stems climbing the walls were not visible from the front of the house. Considering how fast they grew, they must have crept around the side of the house at some point, but his nimble-fingered wife had cut them back in time. Oghi was horrified and raked his wife over the coals for it.

Now that she had been rendered incapable of tending the garden, the trees, grass, and flowers had all died, but the vines on the back wall had grown all the more lush, and their grip was so powerful that they were stretching and spreading around to the front of the house at an alarming pace. Each time the wind blew, Oghi saw enormous ivy leaves shaking outside his bedroom window. He gazed up uneasily at those dark green leaves. It would not be long now before they'd encroached over the entire window and blocked out his view.

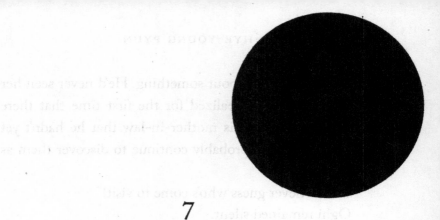

7

Oghi was woken by noise coming from the living room. It sounded like people singing in a low murmur. Wondering what was going on, Oghi tried to summon the caregiver by giving two long blows on his whistle.

"Are you up?"

His mother-in-law came through the door instead. Her voice was loud and cheery. The complete opposite of her usual quiet way of talking or the indecipherable muttering she did when it was just the two of them.

Each time she mumbled, Oghi assumed she was talking to him and tried to catch her eyes, to ask her to speak up. But she never once responded. It didn't even embarrass her to be caught talking to herself. Compared to that, it was much better seeing her as she was today, looking and sounding perky.

She was excited about something. He'd never seen her like this before. He realized for the first time that there were many sides to his mother-in-law that he hadn't yet seen, and that he'd probably continue to discover them as time went on.

"You'll never guess who's come to visit!"

Oghi remained silent.

"Hold on to your hat!"

The only thing that would've sent Oghi's hat flying was if his dead wife had come back to life.

His mother-in-law opened the door and a group of people trooped in and circled Oghi's bed. It was early morning, but they were dressed in black suits like they were on their way to a funeral, and in their hands they carried leather-bound Bibles. They greeted Oghi with smiles. They remarked on how great he looked, on how his eyes shined. It would have made more sense for them to frown or make pitying looks the moment they saw him, but instead their smiles grew wider. Oghi stared at his mother-in-law, asking for her help.

"The pastor is here. He's come to pray for you. I bet if you knew where these kind folks were from, you would hop right out of this bed from surprise."

The people in black laughed uproariously, as if she'd just told some wonderful joke.

"Now, now, you mustn't let surprise lift you," one of the visitors said. "You must let the Lord lift you."

The visitor was a short man whose unnaturally wide grin never once let up. Oghi's mother-in-law explained that he was the pastor.

The pastor held Oghi's right hand, the one that still lacked sensation. He had grabbed his left hand first, but when Oghi's mother-in-law corrected him, he hurriedly switched. At his signal, the people flanking the bed all held hands. His mother-in-law offered them both of her hands as well.

The pastor closed his eyes and began to pray. It was strange. Oghi had never met this pastor before, but he gave a very long prayer, as if he'd known Oghi forever. The pastor spoke of how Oghi had devoted himself to earnest and proper research and education over the years. He said no child of the Lord was kinder, a better family man, or a stronger role model than Oghi. He said the misfortunes that had befallen Oghi were indeed his greatest trial. He said he prayed that Oghi would overcome this ordeal, return to the classroom, foster outstanding students, undertake great academic research, and serve the development and spirit of the country, and in so doing the Lord would use this small but precious nation.

Oghi couldn't take any more and opened his eyes. They were all muttering to themselves or wagging their heads as they participated in this ridiculous prayer to national development. The church people kept blurting out "Father!" as they prayed, and though Oghi knew they weren't talking

about his own father, it still bothered him. Had his father
been there, he would have laughed at Oghi and said, That's
what you get for acting all high and mighty. The pastor's
prayer kept going, and Oghi coughed to signal that he
should stop already. The pastor ignored him and prayed to
his heart's content.

As the pastor closed the prayer with an amen, the circle
of people chanted amen in unison and opened their eyes.
Oghi mouthed his own amen. He had prayed too. Prayed
that they'd hurry up and get the hell out. But Oghi's simple
prayer was not answered. They held hands again, and this
time, they swayed their hands back and forth as they sang.
It was a hymn Oghi had never heard before.

His mother-in-law sang along with them. Oghi was
flummoxed. He wondered if she had always been this
enthusiastic about religion or if it was a recent thing. She
might have started going to church when his father-in-law
passed away a few years ago. She'd become clingier after he
was gone, and Oghi's wife had sometimes struggled with it
and sometimes ignored it. He had often overheard his wife
on the phone with her, his wife's side of the conversation
studded with please don'ts or with flat refusals of whatever
his mother-in-law was proposing. She'd called so often that
sometimes Oghi's wife wouldn't answer the phone at all.
Why hadn't she told Oghi more about his mother-in-law
back then?

The hymn continued on for four verses. Oghi closed
his eyes. He missed his wife. He missed her more than he

could put into words. She was the only person who could have made it all stop. But she wasn't there.

At last the hymn ended and they let go of one another's hands. Maybe it was all the black clothes, but they looked like they were there to deliver a requiem. And maybe they actually were. Maybe they had started early because they were there not for Oghi but for his deceased wife. The singing he'd heard when he woke up was probably a hymn honoring her.

The pastor cracked open his Bible and read from it. Everyone nodded or closed their eyes as they listened. Then they held hands for a third time, swung them back and forth, and sang yet another hymn. Afterward, the pastor took Oghi's hand and gave a short prayer. As soon as he heard the pastor say amen, Oghi's heart was filled with gratitude. It was finally over.

As they filed out the door, Oghi's mother-in-law stuffed a white envelope into the pastor's hand. It was probably an offering. Oghi took a good long look at it. For the first time he wondered where she had gotten the money to pay for his hospital bills and all of the medical equipment he'd needed. How had she gotten access to his and his wife's bank account, and if that wasn't where she'd gotten the money, then how was she affording all of this? She might have received money from his wife's life insurance and Oghi's accident insurance. But even so, how did his mother-in-law collect on insurance that listed Oghi as the beneficiary?

When she stepped outside to see off the visitors, Oghi's caregiver stepped in and began straightening up his room.

"Shoot, that was a lot of money," she said. She removed Oghi's catheter bottle, which was full from the night before, and added, "Am I right? That was all cash. Seems like a waste to me, but I guess it's better than calling in a shaman. Last house I worked at, the shaman came once a month on the dot. And what a mess each time! We had to steam piles of rice cake, buy crates of fruit, find a severed pig's head. . . The walls of that room were plastered with talismans, I tell you. And every one of those talismans costs money. I watched it all. Watched that shaman walk on the blades of a straw cutter, scatter rice grains, pretend to be possessed by some spirit. You know, walking on blades is no big thing. Anyone can do it with practice. But compared to that, I'd say churches and temples are better. At least pastors and monks are tidy, you know. You don't have to cook 'em a bunch of food, no one crowds in to watch, it's quiet."

The second the door opened, the caregiver ceased her tirade. Oghi's mother-in-law's face was still flushed. She looked happy.

"My daughter was so blessed. She was such a good person. To think that a pastor as busy and important as him would come all this way to personally pray for her. This is truly a blessing."

"Is he very famous?" the caregiver asked loudly as she washed out the catheter bottle.

"You have no idea!" his mother-in-law replied just as loudly. "He's a miracle worker. It wasn't easy bringing him here. He's cured a lot of cancer patients with his laying on of hands."

Oghi had guessed correctly. The pastor was from one of those cults or prayer center type places. Not from any proper denomination.

"He agreed to come back often. To pray for you and my daughter."

Oghi blinked at his mother-in-law.

Please don't. Today was enough.

"I know, I know. You don't have to thank me. It's the least I can do."

Oghi opened his eyes as wide as he could. He wanted to tell her he was angry. He wanted to tell her to knock it off, to stop pissing in the wind. What he needed wasn't prayer but steady rehabilitation. Or to just give up now.

"Where is he from?" the caregiver asked.

His mother-in-law answered loudly, excited at the chance to talk about the pastor. She said the pastor's prayer center was not part of any particular denomination but was a kind of Bible reading group for people who "shared the same heart." Oghi had to press down hard on the urge to ask exactly what kind of "heart" those people were sharing. His mother-in-law would not have understood him, and even if he could have gotten the words out, he wasn't confident he could have endured the long, quiet explanation that would've surely ensued.

He found it a shame that they'd had to pay an enormous donation to listen to prayers and hymns from some unidentified religious group. His mother-in-law had not said anything for certain, but it was obvious it was Oghi's money. It irked him to no end to think that the money he'd saved over the years was slowly trickling over to some religious nutjobs, the intentions of whom were murky, via his mother-in-law's hands and without his consent.

Oghi had been a regular sponsor for a long time of third world children through organizations like UNICEF and Save The World. Whenever he heard the occasional news story about the directors of such organizations embezzling or misappropriating funds, he questioned the utility of that sort of indirect philanthropy, but it didn't stop him from donating. He refused to help finance religious or political organizations or individual politicians. He had zero desire to give his money to some baby-kisser or Bible thumper who'd never gone hungry a day in their life or known what it was to be poor or illiterate.

The only person he could talk to at times like this was his wife. Who else would understand the suffering his mother-in-law was putting him through? But naturally his wife was not there, and all Oghi could do was picture her. His wife had always imagined the worst possible scenarios for herself. As far as Oghi was concerned, she was just anxious and overly convinced that the hypothetical sufferings conjured up by her imagination had a chance of actually happening. He blamed it on the fact that, after failing at everything she'd set out to do, she had lost all trace of her cool and laid-back personality, had grown too obsessive in her care of the garden. But not even she could have guessed what future lay in store for them.

After his mother-in-law's morning visits, Oghi spent the rest of his days alone with the caregiver. His mother-in-law had fixed up the spare room next to the kitchen for her. It was a bit far from Oghi's room, which must have been why she didn't always hear him summoning her, no matter how hard he blew on his whistle. Or maybe she pretended not to hear. Either way, she was slow and tactless. It didn't seem like she'd had any formal schooling. His mother-in-law said she'd hired the woman after several rounds of interviews, but she wasn't very reliable. In fact, she was completely unskilled. He had a feeling she was really just a run-of-the-mill housekeeper.

She talked a lot and would chatter away at Oghi, and though she knew he could not respond at all, she would blatantly poke fun at him. "I guess the big bossman has nothing to say to that," or "Bossman's awful quiet today," she would say.

When she grew tired of making fun of him and wearied of being the only one talking, she made phone calls. Oghi could hear every word all the way in his room whether she was on the house phone in the living room or using her own cell phone. He learned a lot about her that way. He knew how much money she contributed each month to the *gye*, or rotating savings group, that she'd joined, how she got along with the person in charge of that group, and what type of gift she was planning to take to her relative's baby's first birthday party, which was coming up soon.

But most of all, he knew all about her grown son. How bright and clever he was when he was younger (where had he gone wrong?), how much time he was wasting just loafing around, how late he stayed up each night playing those computer games. Her voice changed completely when she talked to him. It sounded pleading, and she said things like, Please don't. Sometimes she added a hint of childish coquetry as she said, Please think of your poor mother. And sometimes she threw her hands up and snapped viciously, I don't care if you starve to death, you're not getting any more money from me!

Whenever her calls dragged on for too long, he blew on his whistle. His mother-in-law was the one who'd decided on the whistle. She'd given it to him. Blowing on it twice summoned the caregiver.

She never came the first time he called. He had to whistle several times before she'd finally bother to check on him. He blew it whenever he needed to pee or his head or back itched or his legs ached or he couldn't bear the sweat on his back. He blew it even when that wasn't the case. He blew it when her phone calls seemed to be getting too long and when she cursed at or pleaded with her son over the phone. When he couldn't figure out what on earth she was doing in the other room, and when he heard her eating by herself, he whistled. Because that was what the whistle was for, and she was his live-in caregiver, after all.

The situation was always the same. She would drag her feet down the hallway, but once she'd stepped into the room, she would chuckle, say something like, "Bossman sure likes to toot on that whistle," and then undo the front of Oghi's barely closed pants. Without even bothering to consider why he might have called her in there, she would first wipe down Oghi's crotch with the damp towel she carried. It was always lukewarm. He wasn't sure if it was the temperature of the damp cloth or the fact that she used it to wipe down everything she saw as she walked around the house, but he cringed each time.

Whenever Oghi had a bowel movement on cue right after she had slid the flat bedpan under his buttocks, she praised him and said things like, "*Aigo*, well done!" When he finished swallowing another liquid meal, she patted him on the head. Oghi hated this very much. He was angry at the meanness of the caregiver who treated him like a child.

Twice a day, she turned Oghi on his stomach to wipe his back. To keep bedsores from forming, she spread oil on his skin and gave him a long massage. From the nape of his neck, down his back, past his buttocks, to the ends of his legs. As she massaged his body, she laughed insidiously. The exact opposite of treating him like a child. Sometimes she gave him a smack on the buttocks, and sometimes she toyed with his darkened, shriveled penis. She did it on purpose. Oghi voiced his protests with long, indecipherable sounds.

After the massage, she bent her fleshy body over his to straighten the blankets. It would have been easier for her to just walk around to the opposite side of the bed and do it, but she never did. She leaned over very far each time, and when she did, her pendulous breasts brushed against Oghi. Sometimes she did it while wearing a tank top with no bra underneath and her nipples visible through the fabric. When she wore that shirt, the thick patches of dark hair in her underarms showed as she reached over him. They gave off the damp, musty odor of sweat. She seemed indifferent to the smell of her own body or to the smells coming off of Oghi.

At first Oghi suppressed his anger. Later, he didn't have to. It had been a long time since anyone's flesh had touched his like that, and Oghi found himself overcoming his disgust. That occasional fleeting brush against his body, if he could have touched it, grasped the flesh in his hand, it would have felt plush beneath his fingers and he would have sensed the heat of the blood vessels below the surface, and if he did touch it, it would have twitched and responded—he liked that. Oghi had never been entranced by fleshier body types, but he liked that meaty weight pressing against him.

But that was all. He did not touch the caregiver or caress her. Of course he didn't. He enjoyed it simply because it was another living person, not the body of an alluring woman. The only thing Oghi could do was smell her. Hair laced with sweat, faint traces of shampoo, sour underarms, the lingering of laundry detergent. The scents given off by a living human being. They were completely different from the odors of sweat and urine that came from his own body.

That was all it took to excite him. Seeing her large, erect nipples. Feeling her press gently against him. Catching glimpses of the pale skin at the nape of her neck or the sweat beading along the side of her throat just below the bottom of her curly, thinning hair.

This was not what used to turn him on in the past. The women he'd slept with were all small and slight. Of all the organic parts that made up a body, Oghi especially liked protruding joints and slender, frail-looking bones. When he stroked the silhouette of a bone through its thin layer of flesh, he felt like he was embracing the woman in her entirety.

It made him sad to be enticed by something so different from before. To be turned on not by the scent of a woman but by the familiar smells of everyday life, to be excited not by taut, bare skin but by the sagging, bloated, thickened meat of a person. That was sad. He had never before been tempted by a body like this.

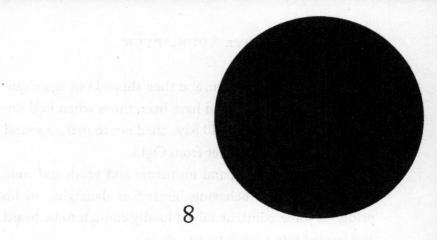

8

His mother-in-law's visits grew more frequent. Before long she was dropping in on him like she lived there. Naturally most of her visits were unannounced. That day was no different. He heard the sound of his mother-in-law opening the front door and stepping inside, followed by the sound of the caregiver coming out of her room then hastily shutting her door and rushing into the living room.

Oghi had not said anything about her to his mother-in-law. He could, with effort, have used his left hand to write a note criticizing the woman's behavior, but that would've been below the belt.

The truth was that he didn't mind any of it. All except for the woman's son, that is, who'd lately been showing up at Oghi's house as well. It was possible the boy had dropped by before then without his knowing about it. He might have come to bum some cash off his mother and eat some food she prepared for him, and then slipped out again quietly. Certainly there would have been times when he'd lingered, but at least he would have tried not to make a sound, to keep his presence secret from Oghi.

But he was young, and immature and brash and rude. Maybe he viewed behaving himself as damaging to his pride. At some point, he talked loudly enough to be heard, and barged into Oghi's room.

When Oghi awoke from his light nap, he was startled and let out a shriek. A young man with darkly bronzed skin and closely cropped hair was standing stock-still and staring down at him with a blank look on his face. His jeans sagged at the hips, and he wore a black T-shirt that read I AM YOUR FATHER.

The caregiver's son laughed at Oghi's reaction. He held his finger up to his mouth as if to swear Oghi to secrecy and left. Oghi heard the caregiver scold her son and ask what he was doing in his room. He heard the boy say, "That guy can't talk?" and the caregiver continue with her quiet nagging.

Oghi was angry and blew on his whistle. Two whistles meant the caregiver had to come. As usual, she didn't. He whistled again. He whistled several times. He kept on whistling. He refused to put up with this. He wanted her to know just how angry he was.

Instead of the caregiver, her son burst through the bedroom door. He looked nothing like his mother. He was skinny to the point of looking sickly, but he was more wiry than frail. He looked like his leanness was due to prolonged suffering. Considering his nearly shaved head and darkly tanned face, he might have just finished his army service.

"Fuck, man, who do you think you are? A drill sergeant? Why do you keep bossing everyone around with that stupid whistle?"

He kicked Oghi's bed. Oghi glared at him, so he ripped the covers off and used his foot to poke at Oghi's numb leg. Oghi's leg must have shook like a twig. The caregiver stood by and watched. The look on her face said there was nothing she could do. Maybe she was enjoying it. She must have been embarrassed, but she showed no intention of stopping her son.

"How would you like it if I used it to order you to stand up? Huh? Would you like that?"

He grabbed the whistle from Oghi and blew on it. At first he blew on it where he stood. But then he held it right up to Oghi's ear and blew. He kept blowing. If the caregiver had not dragged him out of the room, Oghi might have lost his eardrum as well.

"Use your words instead, man. Got it?" he yelled as he was dragged through the door. "We'll be real polite with each other."

Oghi had never felt so scared of a kid before. The students he encountered as a professor had all been raised by well-educated parents. They were well-nourished too, so they were in good physical shape. There were times at the end of the semester when they raised their voices at him and demanded a higher grade in his class, but they were fundamentally conformist and conservative, afraid to rock the boat. There'd been no students like the caregiver's son, so rude and disrespectful, at least not in Oghi's department.

It was the first time since coming home that Oghi had waited eagerly for his mother-in-law. He'd never imagined being terrorized in his own home by someone he was paying to be there. It drove home the fact that his mother-in-law was his only family, and it made him nervous to think what would happen if she were to abandon him.

But though he'd wished for his mother-in-law to intervene, the timing went awry. The person who should have been kicked out was the caregiver's son, not the caregiver.

That day, when his mother-in-law stepped into the house, the caregiver's rush to shut her door seemed to raise her suspicions. She immediately barged into the caregiver's room, fending off the woman's attempts to stop her. A loud racket ensued. Oghi heard a sharp, hysterical sound that he couldn't believe was coming from his mother-in-law, and something else that sounded like the caregiver weeping and wailing.

The two of them carried their argument out of the cramped spare room and into the living room. Oghi could hear their voices clearly now. His mother-in-law was furious. She called the caregiver a thief. The woman feigned innocence, insisting it was a misunderstanding.

"I didn't steal it. The bossman gave it to me. I swear. He told me to keep it."

Oghi's mother-in-law grew even angrier. She demanded to know what on earth she'd done for him that he would have given her this.

"Do you have any idea how much this is worth? Trash like you doesn't deserve this."

The caregiver's tone changed.

"How the hell would I know what it costs?" she snapped. "Let's go in there and ask the cripple. Find out how much he paid for it."

Oghi was shocked. He knew he was a "cripple," saddled with a disability that was difficult to treat, but it was the first time he'd heard the word actually directed at him. What bothered him even more was what his mother-in-law said next.

"You're such trash that you're only good for wiping the asses of cripples."

Oghi closed his eyes. He wished to be no part of any of this. Mud-flinging and hysterics, excuses and lies, stealing—it had nothing to do with him. He didn't need to experience this. But as hard as he tried to convince himself of that, he could not.

His mother-in-law threw open his door. She stomped into the room and held a small ring up to his eyes.

"Look. Look at this."

Oghi closed his eyes, so his mother-in-law grabbed his shattered lower jaw. She would make him look. The prosthesis shook and his jaw ached. She did not let go. No matter how angry she was, Oghi felt she was going too far to be so careless with his injuries.

"Did you give this to that woman? Did you? Tell me."

The ring had a blue stone. His jaw hurt. It hurt so bad his eyes were tearing up. She seemed to notice because she let go then. Oghi's face throbbed.

His mother-in-law had straightened up the house before the caregiver moved in. She'd gathered together all of the jewelry and accessories that his wife had carelessly left scattered around the house. She'd showed the box that held all of it to Oghi. She'd even pulled each item out and displayed it on her palm. There was quite a lot. Some had been gifts, while others were items his wife had bought for herself. Some of it Oghi had bought for her. He couldn't tell what was what. His mother-in-law had said several of the items were very expensive. She'd singled them out and showed them to him, but he did not remember them.

Oghi blinked at his mother-in-law. He kept on blinking. Even though he could shake his head a little and move his left arm, he lay as still as he had when he first awoke from his coma and only blinked his eyes. All while feeling relieved that no matter how hard his mother-in-law grilled him, he was unable to say a single word.

"I knew this would happen. Get out!" she yelled.

Oghi flinched. He thought she was telling him to leave.

"Who do you think you are, stealing from us, getting drunk in broad daylight." She shook her finger at the caregiver.

The caregiver rushed at Oghi. "You crippled son of a bitch, how dare you accuse me of stealing!" She grabbed his numb legs and shook them.

If he'd had any feeling in his legs, they probably would have hurt in her tight grip. But Oghi felt no pain at all. He didn't even flinch. He didn't feel them shake. His body was standing strong against the lies and excuses and misunderstandings. His body held out, but his mood had soured. He'd already been through one terrible accident, and he'd assumed the pain he had to suffer because of it was over by now, but even after all that he'd been through, there was still this endless parade of lies, excuses, misunderstandings. No different than ordinary life. It made no sense.

The caregiver wasn't the one who'd gotten drunk. It was her son. He'd started out cautiously in her small room, and then later drank openly in the living room. When he was good and drunk, he sang loudly and ranted at his mother. He called up places and bitched about his senior officers, and ended his drunken bouts with tears and sobbing. And when he was done crying, he came looking for Oghi, reeking of alcohol. He greeted Oghi, his eyes gleaming in his darkly tanned face.

"I'm sorry, Mister."

He bowed politely from the waist.

"I'm sorry, I drank it all."

He bowed again.

"Goddammit, it was just so good."

Now and then, he would dip the corner of a towel in alcohol and hold it to Oghi's lips. The first time he did this, Ogi had closed his mouth. He didn't want to participate in the boy's mockery of him. But the boy didn't give up. He kept touching the dampened cloth to Oghi's lips until Oghi could no longer resist the peaty aroma of single malt whiskey. How long had it been since he'd had a taste? He was in heaven. The boy gave him a little more, and Oghi stuck his tongue all the way out to lap it up. Later the boy fed it to him with a spoon and even put a straw in a cup for him. The whiskey the boy fed him was good, but it wasn't the best. There were many better whiskies, but either the boy didn't know his whiskies or he'd already drunk them all.

Oghi's mother-in-law went back into the caregiver's room and tossed all of her belongings out into the hallway. The caregiver grabbed whatever she could carry. His mother-in-law threw the front door wide open and chucked the rest of the woman's belongings into the garden. Oghi watched from the window as the caregiver hurriedly stuffed her belongings into a large suitcase.

She was leaving. Now Oghi would have no one to let him smell her skin or to wet his lips with whiskey. A feeling—he didn't know if it was hurt or sorrow—filled his chest. But instead of feeling sad, Oghi told himself that the whiskies the woman's son had drunk were all high-quality single malts. Bottles he'd gone to great effort to bring back from academic conferences and seminars, from his travels, from all over the world. He tried hard to think about how wasteful and annoying it was.

His mother-in-law spent the whole afternoon cleaning out the caregiver's room. She shoved everything the woman had been unable to pack into the trashcan. Then she made several phone calls and informed the people on the other end that she was looking for a new caregiver. She was told over and over by the employment agencies that, unlike hiring nurses by the hour, finding a live-in caregiver was no easy task.

"What can we do?" she lamented to Oghi. "Even if we do find someone, they won't be any better."

That evening, after she left, Oghi was on his own. He was finally alone, just as he had wanted to be when he first returned to this house. It was the first time since waking up from his coma that he was left without a nurse or a caregiver. He thought he would feel free, but he didn't. He was lonely. And frightened and scared. Oghi blew uselessly on his whistle. No one looked in. There was no one to pick on him or treat him badly. No one to yell or get angry at him.

The house was dark. His mother-in-law had been negligent. She had left without turning on any lights. It was stingy of her, and cruel to imply that Oghi wasn't worth the electricity. But then again, it was the first time she'd done this, so maybe it simply hadn't occurred to her to leave one on for him. There wasn't a single light on in the garden either. It would've been nice if she had at least closed the curtains, but because she hadn't, Oghi was left to watch as the world outside the window turned dark, as the branches waving in the darkness looked like someone beckoning to him.

A red light flashed on the nightstand. Someone was calling. If the room hadn't been so dark, he would've missed that faint light coming from the telephone. It did not ring. Come to think of it, the telephone had never once rung the whole time Oghi had been in that room. Perhaps his mother-in-law or the caregiver had turned off the ringer out of consideration for Oghi. Or they might have switched it off since Oghi couldn't answer the phone anyway.

When he looked at the telephone, he got an idea. He groped around in the bed with his left hand and found the back scratcher the caregiver had left there. She'd given it to him and told him to use it whenever his legs itched. Oghi had never once bothered. If he needed to scratch, all he had to do was blow his whistle and summon her.

His idea was to reach over with the back scratcher and use it to pull the phone closer, but it didn't work very well. His left arm almost immediately cramped up. Soon the light stopped flashing. It did not flash again.

Oghi didn't give up. He kept reaching for the telephone. The cord stretched to its limit until he couldn't pull it any closer. He stretched his arm out as far as he could but he couldn't reach the receiver.

After several attempts, he managed to push the speakerphone button with the back of the scratcher. As the dial tone filled the room, his loneliness faded a little. But no sooner did he hear that sound than he hesitated. Even though he could dial, he still couldn't speak. The best he could do was let out an audible sigh. He decided to try anyway. Given the state he was in, anything was worth trying.

There was one phone number he knew by heart. Ever since he'd been able to store numbers in his cell phone, there'd been no further need to memorize them, but this number alone he never forgot. He had deleted it several times from his contacts. He'd made an effort. But those efforts never seemed to last long. The number would spring to mind, every digit, and he would give in. After just a moment's hesitation, he would dial her number, ask her how she was, and listen to her voice. She never called him first. But when he did call, she answered every time.

He used the back scratcher to slowly press the buttons. It took a while for him to press all ten numbers correctly. Finally he heard it ring. It rang for a while. And then she answered. His heart raced. Unlike his wrecked body, his heart was still intact.

He heard her say hello and nearly cried at the sound of that simple greeting. It was such a welcome sound. His heart felt simultaneously relieved and shaken, just like the first time he'd heard someone say she loved him. Hello? There was that voice again. Oghi wanted to speak. He wanted to respond. But each time he tried, a mechanical sound came out.

This time the person on the other end said, Who is this? Pain wracked his chest. He tried again but could only succeed at producing a ragged moan. Oghi was itching to tell her his name. He tried several times. The line was quiet on the other end. He heard the person ask again, suspicion lacing their voice, Who is this? Oghi didn't answer. He stopped trying. It was too hard, there was no point. But he waited without ending the call, in case he got to hear more of her voice. The person on the other end was silent for a moment and then hung up.

The dial tone returned. Oghi felt removed from the entire world. He was even lonelier than before he'd heard her voice.

After a moment, a call came in. This time as well, the phone did not ring. A small light at the bottom flickered. Oghi felt grateful to his mother-in-law. If she hadn't left without turning on the lights, he wouldn't have been able to see it.

He wasn't able to answer on the first try. He moved too slowly and couldn't get his arm to obey his will. Someone had sent him an SOS and he'd missed it. The phone rang again. Oghi hoped the person on the other end had a lot of patience. He narrowly managed to press the button for the speakerphone.

The person on the other end didn't say anything. Oghi spoke as loudly as he could. It sounded like metal scraping over earth. He was out of breath. He thought about how his doctor had told him it would get a little better after his next surgery. His doctor had said that Oghi's voice would be raspy and inarticulate at first, but that he would soon recover normal speech. Oghi was eager to get more treatment and was prepared to endure any suffering if it meant recovery.

"Oghi?"

Oghi heard the sound of his own name.

Yes, it's me.

He tried his hardest to answer. It sounded like he'd said yes. He hoped the other person thought so too.

"Oghi?"

She might not have heard him properly, but it seemed that she knew it was him. He could hear her quiet breaths through the speaker. It sounded like she was crying. His throat closed up. There was still someone out there who cried over him. Oghi wanted to hear that crying sound better. He reached out with the back scratcher and pulled the phone a little closer. It didn't work. He tried again and knocked the phone to the floor.

Oghi couldn't see the phone from where he lay, but it didn't seem to be broken. He could still hear her saying hello through the receiver. Since Oghi couldn't respond, the person soon hung up. The dial tone droned on for a bit, and then even that stopped. All that was left in the room was the dark, which had grown darker still, and the silence.

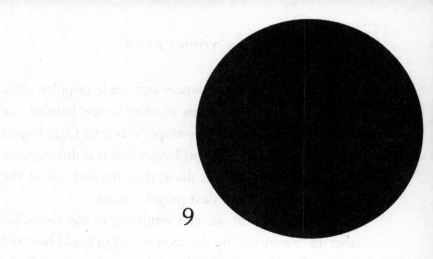

9

His mother-in-law returned around noon the next day, accompanied by the black-garbed church people. When she opened the door, her eyes went to the floor first. She gave Oghi a quizzical look and placed the telephone back on the nightstand.

Oghi's catheter bottle was filled to the brim, so before letting the church people into the room, she emptied and washed it. The church people praised her. Not everyone could handle this sort of work, they said, it takes tremendous love. One of them added, only someone like Jesus himself could do this work.

The pastor held Oghi's hand and prayed, then his followers held one another's hands and sang all four verses of a hymn. This was followed by a sermon, the words of which were slightly different than last time but still no less clichéd. The pastor comforted Oghi and spoke of the miraculous works of Jesus, who cured lepers and made cripples walk. When the praying ended, his mother-in-law handed the pastor another thick white envelope. This time Oghi hoped the pastor would stick around longer, but it didn't happen. As soon as their work was done, they hurried out of the house to go deliver their next prayer session.

After seeing them out and returning to the room, his mother-in-law picked up the receiver. Oghi could hear the dial tone. The phone hadn't been damaged in the fall. As she stood there with the phone in her hand, his mother-in-law fixed Oghi with a suspicious look, then pressed a single button.

Oghi wondered why someone would press only one button on a phone. Of course. The redial button. His mother-in-law shot him another look and wrapped her hand around the mouthpiece. She must have answered. She was probably saying Oghi's name or breathing loudly or crying, as she had last night. Maybe she thought it was Oghi calling and was telling him something right now. His mother-in-law listened silently to the person on the other end.

After a moment, she quietly put the phone back in its cradle and stared at Oghi. He pretended to be sleepy and closed his eyes. He heard her unplug the phone and take it out of his room.

That day, his mother-in-law did not come back to Oghi's room. The catheter bottle filled to the top, and his urine spilled out onto the floor. But he couldn't stop himself from urinating. After the accident, he'd lost the ability to control it. The doctor had explained that the damage to his motor nerves meant he no longer had power over his urethra, and his bladder had shrunk, causing him to urinate more frequently whenever the pressure built up in his abdomen. The tube inserted into his penis dripped continuously like an IV. Maybe it was the medication he was on, but his urine was a darker yellow and smelled worse than usual.

His mother-in-law didn't show up until the next day. This time she arrived carrying a large suitcase. She told Oghi that she would be looking after him for the time being and that she would stay in the room his wife had used as a study.

His wife's room. He could picture it clearly. When his wife wasn't in the garden, she was in that room. Sometimes she had slept in there. Oghi usually let himself in. When it was dinnertime but she still hadn't made any food, when a deliveryman was ringing the bell over and over but she didn't answer the door, when he came home from work but she didn't bother to even peek outside, Oghi went to that room.

She was always seated at her desk. A large bookcase, crammed full of books, stood against the back wall. Whenever she needed to add a new book, she would pull an old one off of the shelves and throw it away. If a new translation of a writer she liked came out, she would find a similarly sized geography book and toss it. Oghi moved his most essential books to his office at the university to keep them out of his wife's hands and kept those he had no choice but to store at home in his own study, but it never failed that unless he was lucky enough to spot one while it was sitting in the recycling bin, his books would find their way out of his life for good.

"Nothing wrong with trimming the fat," his wife would say whenever Oghi asked when they'd become wealthy enough to waste money like that. Each time, his wife had just one objective: to piss Oghi off. She was like that sometimes.

There was a large teak desk in the middle of her room. She had waited three months to put it there. She'd browsed an antique furniture store in Seongbuk-dong every week before buying it, saying she had finally found a desk she liked. It was the most expensive item in their house after the sofa in the living room. More expensive than anything Oghi owned. When he asked her if she really had to have it, she told him she would never have to buy a new desk again. And come to think of it, she was right. She had literally used that desk for the rest of her life.

To one side of the desk was a sideboard that she'd purchased from the same furniture store. On top were souvenirs from her travels and a collection of unusual and expensive picture frames. Only one of the frames held a photo of her and Oghi. It was a snapshot of the two of them riding a tandem bicycle during a trip to Gyeongju that they'd taken back when they were dating. It had obviously been placed there as a reminder of when she'd been young and beautiful and not because it was that special of a memory.

The rest were all photos of women: Susan Sontag photographed by Annie Liebowitz, Virginia Woolf with her hair up, Sylvia Plath at the beach smiling brightly in a white bikini, Tasha Tudor in her garden, Louise Bourgeois in her later years smoking a cigarette, Georgia O'Keeffe with her hair down and the top buttons of her shirt undone, Cindy Sherman in lingerie sprawled on a rumpled bed.

Some were still alive, some were dead. Some had killed themselves, some had died of illness. They were all different, but Oghi soon figured out what they had in common. They were all successful women. Just as his wife had walked around with a photo of Oriana Fallachi in her wallet during her college days, so she had placed these women's photos in her room.

Though in the end Oghi was never able to figure out what kind of work his wife wanted to do, he had a sense of what kind of person she had wanted to become. She didn't want to be a painter or a journalist or an artist or a writer. She had simply wanted to succeed and make a name for herself.

When she wasn't looking after her garden, his wife was shut up in her room with the photos of successful women. Each time Oghi checked in on her, she was sitting at her desk writing something. That was right. She had written something everyday. She wrote on a laptop and in a large notebook. She wrote on Post-its and stuck them to the wall, and she wrote on squares of memo paper and stacked them inside a tin case. Ever since returning the advance for the nonfiction book she'd been contracted to write long ago, she'd stopped talking about writing or showing pages to Oghi, but she had kept on writing.

She mentioned it only once, shortly before their trip. She told him that she'd been working on something. Oghi guessed it was a gardening book.

"Wrong." She answered simply, "It's an open letter."

"Open letter?"

This was interesting. She hadn't written anything like that before. Though, come to think of it, that wasn't entirely true. His wife's first direct sense of the power of words was none other than the open letter she'd written to the boss who sexually harassed her. The first time her writing had achieved something meaningful. The letter she'd posted resulted in her boss being expelled from the press association and compelled the company to improve their working conditions. And it had all started with something she wrote.

"*J'accuse*," she murmured.

"What kind of open letter is it?"

"*The truth is on the march and nothing will stop it.*"

She stared directly at Oghi as she quoted Emile Zola.

If Oghi had asked her which truth was on the march, if he had tried to hear her out, she probably would have told him what was going on, even if she'd only meant the quote as a joke. But his wife's gaze and her mumbling rubbed him the wrong way. He sighed, said, "You're using that quote wrong," and got up and left.

It didn't occur to him until they were in the car on the way to their destination that maybe he should have heard her out. He'd been slow to realize that things between them had gotten to the point that this was the only way she could try to talk to him. As with all things in life, his realization came too late.

Oghi's mother-in-law did not come out of his wife's room for a long time. She'd probably gone in there and looked around at first just to tidy up, but it wouldn't have taken long for her to notice the notes plastered all over the walls, covering the surface of her desk, filling the drawers. His wife had been a compulsive recorder. She not only kept notes on the books she read—title, number of pages, content—she even kept summaries of her phone conversations—who she spoke to, what they talked about.

She was meticulous in her notes on Oghi. She wrote down what they argued about and what kind of promises Oghi made while making up with her. Later she would retrieve the note and stick it in Oghi's face. She would tell him how he'd disappointed her and that he'd made the exact same mistake before. She would get angry and tell him his pledges and promises were useless. Oghi would apologize and make another promise dripping with sincerity. But before long, he'd be subject to the exact same criticism again. Oghi quickly grew sick of it.

His wife also recorded what time Oghi returned home everyday on her desk calendar. He had grown busier and more and more often failed to keep the promises he made to her. More than once he told her they would eat dinner together only to come home past midnight. Though he called or texted plenty to ask for her forgiveness, she got angry each time. When those days added up, she brought out her calendar to show him just how many times he'd broken his promises. Oghi never knew what to say.

At one point, his wife tried to have a baby. She got shots when she was ovulating, took pills, saw the doctor. Several times Oghi went into a little room and, with the help of some videos, extracted his sperm. Several rounds of artificial insemination failed, so they tried in vitro with its slightly better odds. Nothing worked. This had made his wife sad, of course, but she looked like she got over it soon enough. As was her way, she was quick to give up and resign herself.

Nevertheless, Oghi had felt he should comfort her. She seemed to be deliberately masking her depression and unhappiness. She chose cynicism over grief, which he found even harder to stand.

But each time he tried, she mocked him, turned sarcastic. Called him a snob. She was quick to blame him. It wasn't fair. He was doing the best he could. He had worked hard to build up his resume, and that had brought him more work. His wife didn't understand that. He was hurt. Yes, he was building a life for himself, but he'd never thought of her as not being a part of that life. She had to know that.

And of course it didn't mean that she *couldn't* think of herself as separate from him. It just meant that she had to build a life for herself too.

His mother-in-law would find the things his wife had written and would read them all. She would learn all the things her daughter had not told her over the years. From the words she'd jotted down in notebooks, from the even stacks of memo paper, from the Post-its scattered everywhere. His mother-in-law would think the same things about Oghi as his wife had. The same misunderstandings, the same harbored grudges. This filled him with dread.

The next morning she came into his room early. Her face was haggard, like she hadn't slept well, or at all. He tried to read her expression, but he couldn't tell what she was thinking. She sat on a small chair and gazed at Oghi without saying a single word. He grew uneasy. What had she learned about him overnight?

She let out a long sigh and began to speak calmly.

"It's time to rethink things."

Did she know? That had his trip ended safely, Oghi and his mother-in-law might not have been family anymore? It was unfortunate that, of all possible times, she had to find out right when he was without a private nurse. Oghi quickly tried to think of who might help him, besides his mother-in-law. He couldn't think of anyone.

"I mean, just look at the shape that garden is in. It doesn't look like anyone lives here."

She was talking about the garden? But Oghi knew he couldn't breathe easy yet. After all, the garden was his wife's space. That meant she was really talking about his wife.

"But the garden isn't the problem right now. It's not the real problem."

Of course the problem wasn't the stupid garden. The problem was Oghi. Always Oghi. And his recovery.

"I'm talking about money."

Oghi was taken aback. How had he not thought more deeply about that before? It had crossed his mind, just never for long. His mother-in-law had struggled to ask him if she could keep a single ring for herself. Sure, she gave money away to that worthless faith healer, but she still seemed aboveboard and discerning when it came to the subject of money.

"I did the math. This house, your savings, your stocks, my daughter's insurance, your insurance. . . I added it all up."

She tapped at a calculator.

"You've got a lot of debt. This house, I mean. If I deduct that. . ."

She let out another sigh. Oghi had been making interest payments steadily and had paid off most of the house loan. The amount left wasn't as much as she was implying. Whenever other people moaned about how hard it was to make ends meet, he had chimed in and agreed with them and exaggerated how much he was in debt, but in fact he could have paid the rest of the loan off that instant if he had to.

"This is all we have. See that?"

She tapped a number into the calculator and held it right up to his eyes. It was too close for him to read. She jerked it away and let out another sigh.

Oghi paid less attention to how much "all" was than to the fact that she'd said "we." It was obvious she thought of his money as her money too. Even though he was the one who'd worked to save it. He was even the one who'd made the monthly payments on the life insurance policy that had paid out on his wife's death.

"Now let's look at how much money we're spending every month. The fees for your caregiver, the money we pay to your physical therapist, the prayer fees for the pastor, outpatient treatment fees, rental fees for your medical equipment, consultation fees, medication—phew . . . This is how much you're spending every single month. And that's not all. There's also loan interest, maintenance costs on the house, utilities, basic living expenses. . . I mean, there's nothing to cut back on. When I add it all up. . ."

She stuck the calculator in his face again.

"This is how much we need. Don't be shocked. Two healthy people would never spend this much, even if they were living high on the hog."

Oghi couldn't make out a single digit. He didn't bother gesturing with his eyes for her to show it to him again either. He knew she wasn't actually trying to show him the numbers. She just wanted to tell him how much a worthless cripple like him who did nothing but lie on his back all day was costing each month.

But he didn't care. Even if she did think of it as "their" money and frittered it all away. He didn't even mind if she spent all of his money and went into debt paying for his medical care. Even if he lost everything he owned, at least he was alive, and he would get treatment and be rehabilitated, and he would become healthy again. Then he would return to teaching. Get well soon and come back—that's what the dean had told him when he visited Oghi in the hospital.

Once he was able to get around in a wheelchair, Oghi planned to jump right back into teaching. He would have to wait until he got his face fixed and his shattered jaw repaired before he could actually lecture, but he could at least push his own wheelchair with his left hand. At a time when even able-bodied people were sitting around idle, unable to find work, Oghi had a job to return to, even if all he did at the moment was lie on his back without moving. The school had given Oghi tenure. Oghi would complete his rehabilitation, return to the university, and fulfill that tenure.

Once he was able to move his hands freely, he would also be able to write that book on ancient Korean maps that he'd kept putting off before for lack of time. He already had plenty of research material on the subject. Each time he'd traveled to Europe, Japan, or other places, he'd visited libraries and collected material. It was a book that should have been published right away, if only he'd had time to spend writing. He'd simply been postponing it because of his many other activities.

He figured he could also go on the lecture circuit as he had before. His lectures might even make a more stirring impression now. He could tell people how his once healthy body had ended up like this, and how he'd conquered his injuries. The idea cheered him up. It helped him to endure his silent, unmoving limbs.

"I guess we'll have to cut back on your nursing costs."

Oghi wanted to yell that that was absurd. He shuddered at the idea of trusting his body to his mother-in-law's care. He blinked feverishly.

"Yes, yes, I know. It's a big sacrifice for me. And at my age! I'll make myself sick caring for you."

That wasn't true. She was more than healthy. She wasn't the one wasting away, Oghi was.

"But we have to cut back. Wherever we can."

With that, she left the room without a single look back. Oghi lost count of how many times he'd blinked, but she had ignored it. He blew his whistle, but the door did not open again.

He felt like he was rolling downhill, pinned beneath the heavy weight of the car. He was better off then. Back then, he thought it was all over. It had been terrifying, yes, but he'd also felt at peace. This, however, was not the end. This was the beginning of something. He thought he'd already been through a lot, but it seemed there was more to come. And it would be nothing compared to the torment he'd experienced thus far.

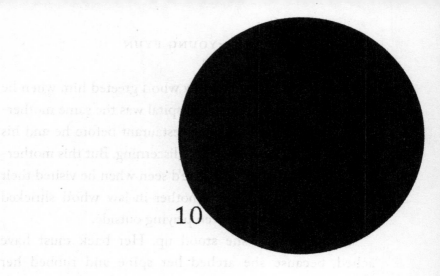

10

W<small>HEN SHE WAS IN THE</small> garden, Oghi's mother-in-law wore
a hat with a brim so wide it nearly covered her whole face.
On her arms were black sleeve protectors, and she wore
pants that tightened at the ankle. She looked exactly like
Oghi's wife used to. Everything she wore had belonged to
her.

Oghi used his left hand to raise the head of the bed
until he was in a half-reclined position so he could watch
his mother-in-law as she worked outside. What was she
doing? He couldn't see her very well from where he sat, but
she seemed to be turning over the soil. She must have had
plans to revive the garden, just as his wife had long ago. She
showed no intention of spending any time filling in for a
caregiver and looking after Oghi properly.

His mother-in-law glanced up at Oghi's window,
turned away with a hard look on her face, and dove back

into work. The mother-in-law who'd greeted him when he woke from his coma in the hospital was the same mother-in-law he'd met at the hotel restaurant before he and his wife got married. Refined and discerning. But this mother-in-law now was the version he'd seen when he visited their apartment in Mapo. The mother-in-law who'd shrieked with no warning at children playing outside.

After a while she stood up. Her back must have ached, because she arched her spine and rubbed her lower back, and then as if to show off her perfectly functional limbs, she stretched them out long and massaged the muscles. She put away the hoe, came into the house, and did something in the kitchen for a long time before finally, finally coming to Oghi's room.

She pulled on a pair of latex gloves and emptied his catheter bottle. The caregiver had done everything with her bare hands, but his mother-in-law took pains not to touch anything Oghi had used, as if afraid she might catch something from him. Then, just as the caretaker used to do, after emptying the catheter bottle, she opened the front of Oghi's pants.

Oghi shook his left hand to tell her no, to make her stop. His hand flapped uselessly, unable to reach her. She paid no attention. He tried to close his legs. He tried to bend his knees. Of course, nothing worked. Helplessly, he shouted as loudly as he could. He wanted her to know that she was making him extremely uncomfortable. It came out as a moan.

She wiped down Oghi's body and connected his feeding tube, all while muttering something. Oghi strained to catch what it was. He thought she was talking to him. He couldn't quite make it out. It was just a continuous mumble. He wondered if she was cussing. Her face was hard, and she looked angry. He wanted her to hurry up and get angry, to give up on looking after him. But no matter how her face hardened, no matter how completely her once sweet and elegant voice went away, she did not raise her voice at him in anger.

While Oghi slowly drank his dinner, his mother-in-law stared blankly into space and murmured something over and over to herself. Oghi still couldn't tell what she was saying. When he'd finished his meal, she stood with a grunt and let out a sigh. Mixed in with the sigh, one phrase suddenly stood out clearly.

"*Tasukete kudasai.*"

Oghi memorized it. He repeated it to himself so as to not forget. *TasuketekudasaiTasuketekudasaiTasuketekudasai-TasuketekudasaiTasuketekudasaiTasuketekudasai.*

The ambulance came in the afternoon. With the orderly's help, Oghi lay on the stretcher and was loaded into the back. His mother-in-law came with him. She climbed into the ambulance and sat on the narrow bench next to the orderly, occasionally reaching over to brush Oghi's sweaty hair out of his eyes.

As soon as they were in the hospital, he felt relieved. He felt he was in a safe place. He greeted the nurses who'd looked after him when he was first hospitalized. They told him he looked much better. They asked if he liked being back home. His mother-in-law smiled and looked back and forth between him and the nurses. He gave them a slow blink.

As the long, boring checkup went on and on, Oghi soon grew tired. His mother-in-law never left his side, despite looking just as tired and worn-out as him. Each time he was moved to a different examination room, she trailed along after the gurney and sat in a chair in the waiting area where she closed her sleepy-looking eyes while he was being examined, only to get up and follow him again to the next room, the heels of her shoes scuffing the floor behind her.

While watching her trail after the gurney, her shoulders sagging, Oghi realized that his mother-in-law had aged greatly. Seeing her in the hospital like this, she wasn't dignified and elegant, nor was she rough and mean. She simply looked like an old woman tired of everything.

His mother-in-law had maintained her youth even after his father-in-law's sudden passing three years earlier due to arrhythmia, but after his wife's death, she seemed to instantly lose her tight grip on life. Before, from certain angles, she could have passed as being in her fifties, but now, with the loss of her daughter, she'd lost her looks too. Liver spots had cropped up along the contours of her face and her white hairs had multiplied, making her hair look ashen, as she never bothered to dye it. Up until then she'd always dressed in chicly monochromatic outfits, but now she wore loose, comfortable, garishly colored clothing.

Oghi thought about how genuinely happy his mother-in-law had been when he was made full professor. Aside from his wife, no one else had congratulated him more. He received almost no congratulations from his colleagues, so when he saw how happy his mother-in-law was, it'd made him realize that they truly were family. After he and his wife married, the words *orphan* and *inferiority complex* never came out of his mother-in-law's mouth again. Instead she told his wife that it "worked out well" for her that Oghi had no close living relatives. When his wife grew depressed from her continued failure to get pregnant, his mother-in-law comforted and reassured Oghi more than her.

His mother-in-law was the only family Oghi had left. And it finally hit him that it was the same for her too. They were each other's sole surviving family members. Of course, had his wife lived, their relationship might have become a non-familial one. That very nearly happened. But not anymore. Oghi and his mother-in-law had lost that chance, and now they were stuck with each other.

Oghi and his mother-in-law were learning the sides of each other that only family would see. His mother-in-law had screamed in front of him and thrown out his live-in caregiver. She had brought in a whole pack of people from some unsavory religious organization and bowed and scraped and showered them with offerings. She muttered to herself constantly in Japanese. Oghi was no better. She had to look after him. She had to wipe his crotch and sprinkle it with baby powder so he wouldn't get a rash. Empty his catheter bottles and wash his bedpan when it was full. Only now that his wife was dead had he and his mother-in-law become true family.

The doctor pointed to the results of the CT scan on the computer and told Oghi that his prognosis was good. If he worked hard at rehabilitation, he would be able to use a wheelchair someday. Oghi wasn't thrilled. What that really meant was that no matter how much better Oghi got, he would still never walk again.

His mother-in-law cautiously asked if that meant he was recovering. In a flat voice, the doctor said it was difficult to be optimistic about his lower body, but there were clear indications that the muscles and nerves in his upper body were improving. He joked that soon Oghi would be able to scratch his leg with his right hand.

"This is all thanks to you, ma'am. Isn't that right, Oghi?"

Oghi stared up at the ceiling in response. His mother-in-law stared vacantly at the doctor. She did not look at Oghi. He'd gotten a clear look at her face right when she heard the doctor say that his prognosis was good. She'd looked terrified. He'd never seen her look that way before. She looked frightened and anxious. Like she was asking herself whether she'd really helped Oghi to get better, whether the son-in-law who'd survived while her daughter died should really get to keep living, whether he really would continue to get better, whether that really was thanks to her. It seemed he would be seeing that look on her face often. That look of fear that Oghi might get better. That look of hope that he would not.

Oghi mouthed the word *paper* at the nurse. The nurse didn't understand. He had to mime writing with his left hand before she finally got it and brought him pen and paper.

The doctor and the nurse did not rush Oghi but waited as he wrote something down. With his violently trembling left hand, Oghi was barely able to scribble a handful of letters.

"Does that say, *surgery sooner?*"

Oghi blinked.

"Why, that's fantastic, Oghi. You must keep writing. That's the only way your left hand will get stronger. You'll build muscle," the doctor said in encouragement. "After your next surgery, you'll be in much better shape. You'll even be able to talk slowly."

That was what Oghi was hoping for. Being able to talk. Not blinking his eyes but really communicating. Right now, Oghi wanted that more than walking.

"That too will take practice. You'll have to relearn everything. It's like being born all over again. Babies take a long time learning how to talk, and they're awkward at first, right? But eventually you'll get better. Naturally you will. Keep up the writing practice. Your right hand will get better too, but you have to keep using the side that's already recovered motor function in order to adjust. Understand?"

The doctor instructed Oghi's mother-in-law to give Oghi pen and paper so they could communicate. She nodded slowly, her face hard.

"Now, let's take a look at the schedule."

The doctor conferred with the nurse. It took them a while.

Once he was able to talk, the first thing Oghi would do was hire a new caregiver. He would stop his mother-in-law from looking after him herself. He would ask a lawyer how to go about appointing a legal representative.

The doctor's calendar was full. The only way to accommodate Oghi was to switch his surgery date with another patient's. It would take some doing, but he offered to perform Oghi's surgery one day earlier.

"Even if it's only one day, would you still like to move it up?" the nurse asked.

His mother-in-law stared at Oghi and said, "What do you think?" She looked tired. Her terrified expression from before, the one he would never forget, was gone now.

His mother-in-law simply looked old. She looked exhausted and worn-out. If she hadn't unexpectedly lost her daughter, she would have been able to take it easy, to grow old with dignity. Just as she'd said, she would make herself sick and waste away to nothing trying to care for her son-in-law. That's how old she was.

Fear washed over Oghi. When he looked at his mother-in-law's tired face, he could not help but acknowledge that he was stuck. Even if he recovered enough to look after himself, he might only be switching places with his elderly mother-in-law. But he was more than willing to do just that.

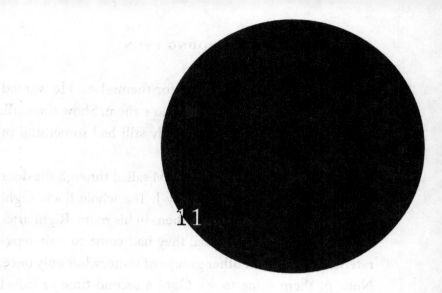

11

BACK WHEN OGHI FIRST AWOKE in the hospital, he couldn't bear the thought of visitors. He didn't want anyone to witness his wreck of a face, the moans that only emerged from his throat with great effort, his petrified tree of a body. It angered him to be in this plight while they weren't. And yet, the idea that no one might come made him even more anxious. And so he saw every single person who came to visit. He saw the dean and the other professors from his department. He saw his old school friends and a whole crowd of colleagues. They all reminded Oghi of where he was supposed to be.

After a little while, he didn't have to think about it anymore because no one came to see him. It was only natural, but he still felt hurt. He sometimes pictured them receiving news of his death. He pictured those who would lament his passing even while feverishly calculating how they could

claim his now vacant position for themselves. He wanted
to get better quickly, if only to show them. Show them all.
That Oghi with his petrified body still had something of
his own while they did not.

What were they doing here? M sailed through the door
first, then S and K, followed by J. The whole flock. Oghi
was shocked to see all four of them in his room. Right after
Oghi awoke from his coma, they had come to visit sepa-
rately, mixed in with other groups of visitors, but only once.
None of them came to see Oghi a second time or called
the hospital to ask a nurse how his recovery was coming
along. Had one of them contacted the hospital or called
the house and gotten permission to visit from his mother-
in-law? Had his mother-in-law not said anything to Oghi
because she wanted him to be surprised?

He was glad to see them. He was happy to know that
they still missed him and that even though they hadn't seen
one another in a long time, they hadn't forgotten him. They
made him believe that despite being confined to a bed and
unable to move, he was still good for something. At the
same time, the sight of their healthy selves, intact and ener-
getic, took the wind out of him. He wasn't crazy about having to see them face-to-face. In fact, he wished they would
all leave right now. It was a shame they had to see him like
this, no more recovered than before.

Back when M had visited him in the hospital, he'd held
Oghi's left hand for a long time. S and J had put up a good
front at first, but when they found out he couldn't speak,

they'd sniffled like babies. K had struggled to stay cool and hide his expression. They had all done their best to avoid looking at Oghi.

"He says he's been waiting forever. What took you so long? He missed you all."

His mother-in-law was putting words in Oghi's mouth. Oghi hadn't said a thing. He was conscious of the prosthesis holding his jaw in place. If he opened his mouth carelessly, a long thread of drool would spill out.

The four of them stood in a row at Oghi's side. He was nervous. He felt no different from when he was surrounded by the black-garbed people who'd come to pray. They were there for him, but he couldn't help feeling like he'd become a laughingstock.

All Oghi did was blink, but his mother-in-law invented words for him as she pretended to interpret. She asked them how things were at the university and said things like, It's the middle of the semester, isn't this a busy time for you? After a few clipped questions and answers, she abruptly changed the subject and said, "Don't just stand there like you're going to run off at any second, here, have a seat," and offered them folding chairs. This time, at least, her translation wasn't far off the mark, and so Oghi blinked.

His mother-in-law's appearance was sloppier than usual. She'd been wearing his wife's clothes while staying at his house, but today her outfit was especially wrinkled and there was a large stain on the front of her shirt. His mother-in-law was fleshier than his wife, so the sleeves were too short, and each time she bent over, the thick rolls of fat at her waist bulged out.

"He wants to know if you had any trouble finding the house."

M replied that they had been there before.

"Ah, that's right," she muttered, staring at Oghi. "You have."

That reminded him that they were the same guests who'd come to his last barbecue long ago.

His mother-in-law apologized, saying she should offer them something to eat but with the house in such awful shape she'd had no time to prepare anything. The four waved their hands and said of course that wasn't necessary.

"If you've been to the house before, then that must mean you had a barbecue out in the yard. With drinks."

"Oghi did all the barbecuing," S said.

"Any idiot can work a grill." His mother-in-law's voice turned sharp.

"But not everyone can do what you do," M said, sounding overly cheerful as he tried to ease the sudden tension in the room. "Taking care of Oghi all on your own. You're amazing."

K and S rushed to flatter her too. They told her how young she looked and how pretty she was.

"But you're not Oghi's mother, you're his mother-*in-law*, right?" J asked.

Oghi's mother-in-law stared at her. M and K laid it on thicker and said, "That makes you even more amazing!" She let out a loud laugh.

"Mother, mother-in-law, what's the difference? It's all the same to him. After all, I'm all he's got. Isn't that right?"

Oghi avoided her eyes. She paid no mind and kept going.

"Truth is, he and I are in the same position. I'm a widow, he's a widower. Misery does love company."

The four of them smiled awkwardly and didn't respond. They seemed unsure as to whether she was joking or not.

"Widows and widowers aren't just to be pitied. Once you experience it, you find it has its good sides. Do you know what the best part of being a widow is?"

She looked around at them. Even S, who normally had so much to say, was keeping his mouth shut and trying to read her mood.

"Your husband can't cheat on you anymore. A dead husband is so much better than a cheating husband."

She let out another loud laugh and stared at Oghi. She was clearly enjoying herself. Oghi frowned. His skin was so scarred that the frown probably didn't show very well, but he did his best. He wanted the four of them to know that he did not agree with her.

"So, do you know what the best part of being a widower is?"

The four of them stayed silent this time as well. His mother-in-law said to Oghi, "It'd be better if you could tell this one," and then answered her own question.

"You can fuck whoever you want and it's not cheating."

She burst out laughing again. She laughed so hard that she had to wipe away her tears. The four visitors acted as if they hadn't heard her.

"Oh, but where are my manners," she said, as she struggled to stop laughing. "I haven't given you anything to eat or drink."

"Oh no, please don't go to any trouble on our account."

"It'd be nice to have a barbecue today, but as you can see, the garden is a mess."

"It looks like you're planting something," S said.

"I have to. Because it's dead. Dead and gone. All of it. . . Raised with so much love and care, only to die for no reason." She paused before continuing. "I have to bring it back to life. I have to. I have to save it."

"You're planting a tree?"

"Trees? Yes, I should plant some."

"You must be planting a big tree. That hole is enormous."

"I have a long way to go. I have to keep digging."

"It must be a really huge tree then."

"It's not a tree. It's a pond."

"A pond? In the front yard?"

"So I can release something living into it. Fill it with something alive, something that breathes and swims and flicks its tail at everything that catches its eye."

"Are you talking about a koi pond? That sounds wonderful."

"Are living things wonderful? They're filthy and disgusting. They'll scrabble like crazy to try to survive inside that cramped hole. . ."

Her sharp response made S stop asking questions. Oghi blinked at him. He was trying to tell him to knock it off, but S turned away and pretended not to notice. He didn't ask what Oghi was trying to say either. He acted like Oghi wasn't even there.

"Even in a dead end place like that, they still cling to life." K tried to take over from S.

"Aren't ponds usually placed at the edge of a yard?"

"You don't know what you're talking about. It has to get a lot of sun. And good airflow. That's why the pond is where it is."

K stopped talking as well. He seemed to realize it was better to keep quiet.

"I'll bring you all some juice."

"That's okay, we just came to see Oghi." M tried to dissuade her.

"Oghi says I absolutely must give you something to drink. Isn't that right? That's what you're telling me, isn't it? He says he wants you to enjoy yourselves while you're here."

She rushed out of the room. They heard rattling and slamming coming from the kitchen, and what sounded like glass or porcelain being pulled from the cupboards.

The four of them glanced at one another, identically ill at ease, but no one spoke. His mother-in-law quickly returned carrying a large tray. On the tray was a bottle of whiskey and four glasses.

"My, oh my, I've been so behind on my housekeeping that this is all we have. I didn't realize we'd run out of juice. I'm so sorry about that. And I can't just serve you plain water. You'll have to have this instead. Here, I'll pour you each a glass."

M awkwardly took the glass of whiskey Oghi's mother-in-law offered him. He looked like he thought he had no choice but to go along with it. The others followed suit.

The whiskey was cheap. No matter how much alcohol the caregiver's son had drunk, there had to have been plenty of good stuff left still, but his mother-in-law seemed to have deliberately chosen the cheapest bottle. There was no way that Oghi had bought it for himself; it was probably a gift from a student who didn't know good whiskey from bad.

The four of them each accepted a large tumbler sloshing with whiskey. At his mother-in-law's urging, they even raised a reluctant toast. Fancying herself his interpreter, each time they gave her an awkward look, she emphasized that this was what Oghi wanted.

"What about you, miss? You look like you can drink a lot," she said to J.

J's glass was just as full as when she'd received it.

"Actually, I can't."

"There's nothing to it. Just drink until you feel good. Then you start getting drunk, and getting drunk leads to leaning on someone, and leaning on someone leads to hugging and. . ."

She burst into laughter again. Everyone struggled to laugh with her, but J's face hardened.

"I don't know what I'm talking about. This is what happens when you get old. You don't hold back, you stop watching what you say. . ."

She told them to enjoy themselves and left the room. The faces of Oghi's four visitors softened, as if now they could relax.

S began talking. At first it was various news related to the university that he'd wanted to pass along to Oghi, but soon the four of them were talking only among themselves. Oghi watched as they busily chatted away without regard for him. None of them showing him any consideration.

S started to say something but stopped short and threw a glance at Oghi. He didn't hide the uneasy look on his face. J avoided Oghi's eyes too. She acted as if she was not going to look directly at him at all. He opened his eyes wide. He wondered what S was about to say. At the same time he didn't want to know. Whatever it was would clearly upset him.

While S struggled for words, K said, as if to change the subject, "Our department is very worried about you."

Oghi blinked slowly. K didn't stumble like S did. He simply said what he'd come to say and did not hide the fact that he was now in a position to be able to catch Oghi up on department affairs. K had finished what S was afraid to say.

As soon as he understood what they were telling him, Oghi got angry. He was furious at the world for rolling on its merry way, unscathed and at peace. While he was lying there with his face torn and his body shattered and broken, everyone else was living their lives and rubbing his nose in it. Oghi's injuries had not disturbed their world in the slightest. The only one lying in bed all day, pissing himself, sweating, shitting, worrying about bedsores, then actually getting bedsores, feeling constantly stoned from his meds, drowsy all the time, and watching his life slide by while all he could do was stare up at the ceiling was Oghi. Their lives were free of car accidents and unexpected handicaps. It had happened to Oghi alone. Oghi's world was the only one that collapsed, Oghi's life was the only one that got ripped to shreds.

The tension in the room was thick; everyone had polished off their glasses of whiskey and was sitting there in dumb silence. Oghi had to do something. He couldn't just fume. The four of them would leave any minute now.

Oghi mouthed the word *paper* at J and mimed writing with his left hand. She pulled a small notepad and a pen out of her bag and helped steady his hand as he spelled out something. K watched nervously as Oghi's hand moved across the paper.

This might be his only chance to write something down. His mother-in-law would not give him much more time. There was so much he wanted to ask and so much he wanted to write, but there was one phrase that stood out before the rest. It had not just occurred to him by chance. He'd been repeating it in his head the entire time.

S studied Oghi's scribbles and recited each letter, checking his reaction to see if it was correct. Once Oghi had the first part down, he read it out loud as K filled in the rest.

"*Tasukete kudasai*?"

Oghi blinked. He made an OK sign with his left thumb and forefinger to indicate that K has guessed correctly.

"Save me? Help me?" K asked, looking puzzled. "*Tasukete kudasai* is Japanese for 'save me.' Is that what you meant to write?"

They all stared at Oghi.

M said, "What are you saying? What do you mean by 'save me'? Write some more." The look on his face had turned serious, and he gestured for Oghi to keep going.

Oghi couldn't write anything. There was too much to write. He had to think about what it meant that his mother-in-law had been mumbling the words "save me" the whole time. Was she referring to Oghi's crisis? Was she saying the situation has grown so desperate that she needed help? That didn't seem to be the case. Maybe it was just a habit of hers. Why on earth was she constantly muttering those words?

Oghi didn't have long to mull it over before his mother-in-law came back into the room. J hurriedly put the pen and notepad back in her bag.

"Oh my, look at that. We have to take care of that right away, even if we do have guests over. Please excuse me, this will only take a moment."

His mother-in-law wasn't wearing latex gloves this time as she reached under the bed to remove the catheter bottle. The urine, which was so dark that it looked like food coloring had been added to it, sloshed out of the top.

The four visitors seemed to realize at once what the smell was that had been floating in the room all that time, but they were careful not to show it on their faces. Oghi scowled hard. He wondered if his shredded skin gave any expression to what he was feeling. The sound of his mother-in-law dumping the contents of the container into the toilet and noisily washing it in the sink carried all the way down the hall to them.

She put the washed container back under the bed and, with everyone still in the room, opened the front of Oghi's pants. Oghi raised his left hand to try to stop her. She pinned his hand down with one arm. J let out a quiet shriek and turned her head. Oghi's mother-in-law wiped Oghi's crotch and the tip of his penis where the catheter tube entered, as if it were no big deal, first with a damp washcloth and again with a dry towel.

"We can't let a sick person go uncared for, now can we?" she said.

J glared at Oghi's mother-in-law, her face stony. His mother-in-law blithely finished up her task.

With the front of his pants wide open, Oghi willed himself not to pee. But this time as well Oghi's fervent wish was not to come true. The *plunk, plunk, plunk* of Oghi's urine as it beaded at the end of the catheter tube and dripped into the empty container was all too loud and clear.

Oghi closed his eyes. Only after his mother-in-law had finished everything she wanted to do did she let go of his left hand. The four guests just stood there. No one spoke.

After a long silence, J said, "We better go."

The other three hurriedly stood, as if they'd been waiting for those words, and said goodbye to Oghi. It was the usual clichés. They hoped he'd get better soon. They would visit him often.

Oghi lay there. He didn't look at anyone. He felt ashamed of the way he had greeted them so happily when they first came in, opening his eyes wide, rolling his eyeballs around, groaning.

His mother-in-law led the way to the front door. J started to follow them out of the room but turned at the last second, rushed back to Oghi's side, and whispered in his ear.

"Your mother-in-law invited us here. She called me."

Oghi grabbed J with his left hand. He held on tight. Slowly, he said, *Come. Back. Again.* Had she understood? J nodded.

They had no time to say anything else. His mother-in-law returned to the room to find out what was keeping J.

She stared hard at J, who was just that moment stepping away from Oghi.

When she left the room, his mother-in-law asked Oghi, "Did you say your goodbyes? Who knows when you'll see them again. Don't worry, I'll see them out."

As she was closing his bedroom door, she added one more thing.

"By the way, I submitted your letter of resignation to the school. Don't you think it's a little unfair to your students? There's no telling how long it'll take you to recover. Your students deserve to be taught by someone who's capable."

She slammed the door behind her.

Oghi watched through the window as his visitors walked out the front gate. After they were gone, the iron gate was shut tight.

His mother-in-law did not come inside right away but stood and looked around at the holes that now pockmarked the garden. She turned and looked in Oghi's direction. The darkness was turning his mother-in-law's face pitch-black. She stood there a moment and glared at Oghi, and then hopped like a child along the paving stones that he and his wife had placed in the yard and came inside.

Oghi and his mother-in-law were alone in the house. It would be that way for a long time to come. His mother-in-law knew a lot of things. She did not hide it from Oghi. For all he knew she might have learned all of the things that his wife thought she knew. The problem was, Oghi had no idea what on earth his wife had known.

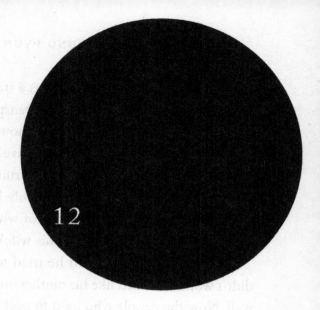

12

THE WORKERS SHOWED UP IN the morning. But it wasn't until they reappeared next to the front gate that Oghi realized they had uprooted the camphor tree planted at the side of the house. It was the same tree that the nursery owner had warned them was not a good fit for such a small yard. But Oghi's wife had been stubborn.

The branches had grown quite dense, just as the nursery owner predicted, but the soft curves nicely complemented the straight, square lines of the house. Despite the concerns, the tree grew thick and healthy and put out lots of soft, green leaves.

The workers replanted the tree next to the front gate. Next to the camphor tree they planted two magnolias so close together their branches touched. Though they weren't as big as the camphor, the magnolia trees also had thick trunks and dense branches. Even Oghi, who knew nothing about growing trees, thought it was a strange arrangement. It looked like the trees had been transplanted not to give them room to grow but to hide the house from view.

Perhaps he was being too negative. Out in the countryside, it was common to see large fruit trees planted next to a house's front gate. Maybe it only looked odd to him because his mother-in-law's idea of what a garden should look like was so different from his wife's.

But no matter how hard he tried to see it that way, it didn't work. It looked like his mother-in-law was building a wall. Now the people who used to peek over the low metal fence and gaze around at the garden would see nothing but tree trunks. More than that, Oghi would see nothing but trees. He would be unable to watch, albeit from afar, as his neighbors walked by. He would not get to enjoy seeing the peddlers' trucks coming to sell fruits or vegetables and the neighbors crowding around them.

Even after the workers left, his mother-in-law was still doing something in the garden. From his window, Oghi couldn't see where she was or what she was doing. He could only make out a few sounds. The sound of something sharp pounding the hard earth, the sound of dirt being dragged up, the sound of the ground being struck with a shovel.

Every now and then he didn't hear anything at all. It got so quiet that he wondered if she had left, and he strained his ears all the more, wondering if she was inside the house. He tried to guess where in the house she was, what she was doing there. Then, as if to mock him, the sounds would start coming from the garden again.

When she opened the gate for the physical therapist, his mother-in-law was the spitting image of Oghi's wife. She was wearing the same clothes and hat that his wife had worn while working in the garden, and she was carrying the same shovel.

As soon as the physical therapist came into his room, Oghi asked for pen and paper. When he tried to voice the words, he failed, but he was able to get his message across by mouthing it. The same trick never worked with his mother-in-law. She always responded as she saw fit.

Take me to the hospital.

"The hospital?"

Oghi blinked.

"Why? Is something wrong?"

He blinked again. He hoped the therapist would start talking and eventually stumble across what it was Oghi wanted to say.

"As a matter of fact, I was planning to tell your mother-in-law that I have to come more often. The thing about rehabilitation is that you can't just do it like we've been doing, where I show up once or twice every now and then. It absolutely will not work. You won't get better that way. I'm guessing you know that too, right? I bet you don't feel that you've made any progress. I'm right, aren't I?"

Oghi blinked.

"But I think your mother-in-law might be having second thoughts."

This was what Oghi wanted. To talk about his mother-in-law.

"The truth is, my house calls are a little pricey. I'd love to offer my services for less, but given my level of experience, my dedication, and my reputation, I've had to raise my prices. I can't just give discounts whenever I want. There are rules about this sort of thing. If I lower my rates, then later I get an earful from my partners. You're probably wondering how they even find out about it. It's crazy, but they know everything. It's because this type of work is all about word of mouth. When one client tells someone else about me, they always mention how much I charge. Even after I've told them that that price is just for them and to please not tell others. That's what burns me up the most."

Oghi mouthed the word at him again: *HOS-PI-TAL.*

"I know. I'm not surprised you would think that. That doing this at the hospital instead with proper equipment would help you get better faster. But you already saw what it's like there. You got physical therapy while you were hospitalized. Ten patients, but only two people to take care of them, right? That's so unacceptable. Injured people are vulnerable! They're each hurt in different ways, and the body parts that need rehabilitation are completely different. For example, today I brought a grip strengthener. You have to use this because the muscles in your right arm are weak. And remember how I put braces on your feet last time? You need those to maintain the right position while exercising the joints. See, it's this kind of thing. The details, the little things you don't notice. Only people with a lot of experience know how to use these tools. But they don't do that at the hospital. You saw that yourself. You broke a blood vessel in your thigh during physical therapy there, didn't you? That's bad. That therapist really messed up. For someone like you, since you don't have any sensation in your joints, if you push it too far, you can pull a ligament. You can even end up with a condition called heterotopic ossification. You may not realize it, but I'm always thinking about you. And not just while I'm here. Before I show up, I think about what to do for you, and when I leave, I think about what to do next time. You have to keep working on strengthening your upper body. That doesn't mean giving up on your lower body. Please don't misunderstand me. I just mean we have to give a chance to the parts that have a chance first. That's why I've had you working your traps, your lats, the muscles in your neck. It's gotten easier to move your head, hasn't it? So when you keep saying 'hospital, hospital' like that, it really hurts my feelings. It costs a lot of money to keep going to the hospital. You have to reserve an ambulance each time, and the orderlies have to come too. It's a lot of trouble. When you compare it to those costs, my services are cheap."

Oghi had no choice but to listen to his whole long, boring speech. It was no use waving his left hand or trying to shake his head to show that wasn't what he meant. The therapist stubbornly shot down Oghi's attempts at communication.

"As a matter of fact, I've been very worried about the fact that you haven't made any progress. I'm supposed to be helping you get better. It must be my fault that you still have no strength. It might not look like it, but I feel really responsible. Once someone is in my care, I'm responsible for them all the way to the end. If I could, I would have you up on your feet this very second. I mean it."

Oghi stared at him. If he could have spoken, he would have said thank you. His therapist had not neglected Oghi. He was doing his best to convince Oghi of that. He seemed to think Oghi was the one calling the shots.

"If you aren't happy with me, please say so. The truth is, exercising the joints can be very painful. In your case, because there's no sensation at all, you can't tell whether or not I'm doing a good job. But you have to trust me. Massages can hurt too, and you can't do it too hard. You have to do it carefully, not use too much pressure, be gentle but stick to technique. That's how I do it."

The therapist was blatantly pleading his case.

Oghi asked for paper again. The therapist hurriedly opened his notepad. Oghi was anxious. This was the only person left besides his mother-in-law whom Oghi got to see now. This time, Oghi wrote *M.I.L. PROBLEM*. It took him a long time just to write those few letters. The therapist had trouble figuring out the second word and kept cocking his head to one side then the other.

"I'm guessing M.I.L. is mother-in-law, but what does this say? Program? Problem? Progress?"

Oghi mouthed the word at him.

"Oh, *problem*, 'mother-in-law problem.' As a matter of fact. . ."

Oghi started to feel relieved. It seemed the therapist knew that she was up to something. He had been there on a relatively regular basis and had stayed for two to three hours at a time. He had witnessed Oghi's neglect and the dark changes to Oghi's house, and had to have a better sense than anyone else that something was amiss.

"It really is a problem."

Oghi nodded.

"I bet you don't know. Out in the yard. She's been digging a really enormous hole. Can you see it from here?"

He went to the window. He stood as far to the right of the glass as he could and said, "You can barely see it from here. The pit. It's huge. . ."

Everyone had mentioned that pit. How big it was, how deep it was, how hard his mother-in-law had been digging away at it.

"She has been acting strange lately."

Oghi was grateful to his therapist for recognizing that much.

"I think she's at it everyday. She ought to rest . . . When I came in earlier as well, she was dripping with sweat as she dug. Have you noticed? She's lost a lot of weight. There might be something wrong with her health too.

A person her age sweating that hard, she'll make herself sick."

Oghi waved his hand to say that wasn't what he'd meant, but the therapist wasn't looking.

"So you're worried about your mother-in-law and you think she needs to go to the hospital? I'll tell her you said that. I'll tell her you're worried about her. I told her myself that she shouldn't work so hard. She could just hire workers instead. She could even ask me for help. I mean, I do get paid by the hour, but if she tells me what's going on, I could knock a little off."

Oghi wanted to exhale. He wanted to expel all the air until his lungs were completely flat. He wanted to rid his body of every last bit of breath.

"I don't know how she intends to dig such a huge pond all on her own. She's going to get hurt overexerting herself like that. When I saw her, she looked like she was in worse shape than you. The elderly can pass away very suddenly, you know."

The therapist slowly massaged Oghi's body. Oghi looked down at his old tree of a body and raised his left arm and bit it hard. It didn't hurt. He bit it some more. He kept biting. No matter how he tried, he could not flex his lower jaw any harder. This time, he struck his left arm against the metal rail on the side of the bed. It hurt. He hit it again harder. If the startled therapist hadn't stopped him, Oghi might have kept beating his arm against the railing until the bone broke. His forearm was red and swollen. He liked that. His body feeling pain and responding to it. Knowing that was the extent of the pain he could feel.

Afterward, on his way out, the physical therapist spoke with Oghi's mother-in-law in the garden. The look on his face was polite and cheery, and he kept bowing. Finally he took out the notepad and showed her what Oghi had written. Oghi's mother-in-law looked at it, and while the therapist was prattling on, she stared up at Oghi's room.

When he heard his mother-in-law enter the house, Oghi let out a long breath. Soon she was in his room and coming toward him without turning on the light. The darkness made her bigger.

"Thank you," she said, her voice raspy.

In the low light, the round flesh beneath her marionette lines drooped.

"I didn't know you were so concerned about me. So you're worried I'll overwork myself and go to an early grave? Look at the shape you're in, and yet you worry about me. Thanks a lot. But you should tell me these things yourself. Then I would be more thankful, wouldn't I? What's this you wrote?"

She held the crumpled paper up to his eyes.

"*M.I.L. PROBLEM.* Right?"

She glared at him quietly in the darkness. Oghi kept repeating the phrase that he'd started muttering to himself some moments before. *TasuketekudasaiTasuketekudasaiTasuketekudasai.*

"People might misunderstand. They won't be able to tell from looking at this whether you meant to say that your mother-in-law *has* a problem or that she *is* a problem. And if she *has* a problem, then is it a physical problem or a mental one? There's no way to tell. I guess you still don't know. What it is I want, I mean. I want you to get better. What else could I possibly want? That's what my daughter would've wanted. So that's what I'll do. What my daughter couldn't. What she meant to do. What she wanted to do. I have to do it for her. And I will. You know she was all I had."

His mother-in-law's rush of words broke off as she burst into tears. She wept loudly like a child. It'd been a long time since he'd seen her cry. He felt sorry. Had he simply misunderstood the ramblings of an elderly woman who'd lost her daughter? Sometimes she looked so frail and unhealthy. So much so that Oghi's suspicions, his animosity, seemed undeserved. Like right now.

But not always. Most of the time, she acted in ways that made it only natural for Oghi to feel afraid and anxious. She didn't seem to be wishing solely for Oghi's recovery. The physical therapist had told him to use a wheelchair. He'd said that if Oghi was to recover functionality in his right arm, not just strengthen the muscles of his left arm, then he had to keep exercising both no matter how hard it got. But Oghi's mother-in-law had said no to Oghi using a wheelchair. There were too many doorsills in the house that would prevent the chair from entering, and it was physically too difficult for her to put Oghi in the chair herself or to take him outside. So the therapist accepted this, and Oghi did not leave his bed.

His mother-in-law also did not use any of the massage methods the therapist had taught her. They were intended to prevent bedsores and keep his muscles supple, but she said it was impossible for her as her arms were simply too weak and she couldn't execute the techniques correctly. The therapist said that made sense. He said it was the new caregiver's job to receive that sort of training. But the new caregiver never came. Perhaps she never would.

His mother-in-law kept forgetting Oghi's meal times. She hardly ever gave him his medication. There were times when she gave him his formula in the morning and then didn't look in on him until very late at night. Each time, she muttered loudly under her breath that she had been so busy working all day she hadn't even realized she was hungry. She clearly meant for him to hear it.

As he watched his mother-in-law's tears stop, her face turn mean, and her glare return, he regretted having momentarily felt sorry for her.

"My daughter was all I had, and I'm all you have. You better not forget that," she snapped, and left the room.

Oghi stared up at the ceiling in the dark and wondered whether J would come back. She had promised, and she always kept her promises. In a few days, he would go back to the hospital for his operation. There, with the nurses' help, he would call J. She would help him. He would consult with a lawyer and appoint a new legal guardian.

But it was never to happen. J did not come back. Oghi spent those days staring out the window, watching for signs that anyone was approaching the gate. But the only person he saw coming or going was his mother-in-law making trips to the supermarket.

Maybe J had misunderstood Oghi. Or maybe she was still deliberating when to come back, who to come back with. Thinking about it that way reassured him. When he imagined J not coming at all, he couldn't take it.

The day of his scheduled hospital visit came, but the ambulance that was to take Oghi there never arrived. Oghi's whole day was a repetition of feeling his mood lift when he heard a car pass by out on the road past the gate with its veil of trees, only to be disappointed again when the car kept going. Not one of the cars stopped in front of the house. The clock ticked past midnight, and still no one came. The headlights of passing cars penetrated the dense row of trees now and then, but none of the headlights were coming to get Oghi.

It was well into the afternoon of the next day when Oghi's mother-in-law came to empty his catheter bottle. He mouthed the word *hospital*. She stared down at him. He mouthed the word again carefully.

"I didn't say anything because I didn't want to disappoint you. Your doctor was in an accident. A car crash. I got such a shock, I can't even tell you. Somehow it never occurred to me that doctors can also get sick or injured. They say doctors can get cancer and Alzheimer's too. Of course, it makes sense. Working in medicine can't prevent you from getting sick. But can you imagine? What if a doctor had a stroke? Or imagine a surgeon having a stroke without realizing it while he's cutting open a patient. Awful. As you know, you can't switch to a new doctor just like that. But at least he says the accident wasn't that bad. I assume that means he's able to walk, unlike you. But he did say he needs treatment. Which means of course that yours has been delayed. He says it'll take him twelve weeks to recover. Probably means he can't operate until then. How can he use a scalpel if his hands are shaking? He could kill someone. So I told them that was okay. I suggested we postpone your operation. And anyway, it's not like your life is hanging in the balance. It's not like someone is going to die if we don't get you that surgery immediately. You certainly won't die without it. You'll still be alive twelve weeks from now. Won't you? Imagine that—you'll still be alive and not dead no matter how far we push back the surgery. How wonderful is that?"

Oghi wanted to argue with her, to say, isn't that too much of a coincidence? But it went without saying that it was possible. It had happened before. Though it was difficult to believe it was happening to Oghi again.

It had happened a long time ago. Just before their second in vitro procedure, their attending physician was in a car accident. Oghi's wife had taken the hospital's advice and changed doctors. She had pushed ahead with the procedure on schedule, but it failed. On top of which, she'd had a very unpleasant experience. The new doctor got inappropriate with her, and Oghi's wife took deep offense. Afterward she refused to go through the procedure again. She gave up on having a baby. She had probably told his mother-in-law about it. She would've been heartbroken and wanting to say that her infertility was not her fault.

"About your physical therapist. I told him not to come for a while. He talks too much. He gets paid by the hour, and I've caught him several times just sitting around talking. We can't keep putting up with it. He just wants to run up the clock. That won't do. I guess we'll have to look for someone who's more trustworthy."

She had said the same thing when she fired the care-giver. That she would look for someone new. But no one had come looking for a job, and she hadn't tried to find anyone.

Oghi had lost his caregiver and now his physical therapist. And that wasn't all he had lost. He had worked so hard, never knowing he would lose everything.

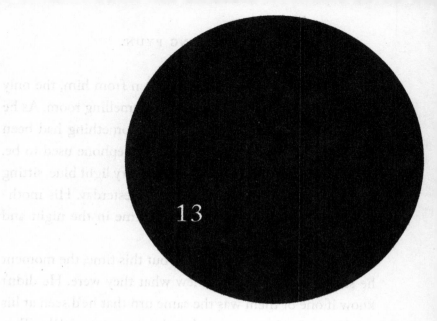

13

THE MAN OUTSIDE THE WINDOW nearly fell off his ladder when he saw Oghi. He must have thought the room was empty. Oghi watched as the man installed security bars, a standard metal grid that bolted in place. The space between the bars was very narrow. Was his mother-in-law having them installed on the off chance that Oghi might try to escape out the window? The idea bothered him greatly, but he also regretted the fact that it had never even occurred to him to try.

The man went away, and this time Oghi's mother-in-law appeared. She lifted the vines that trailed every which way below Oghi's windowsill and wrapped them under and over, through and around each of the iron bars. Given the warmer climate lately, Oghi's window would soon be covered in vines.

Now that even his view was taken from him, the only thing Oghi had left was this familiar smelling room. As he looked around at it, he noticed that something had been placed on the nightstand where the telephone used to be. There were two lidded vases, tinted a very light blue, sitting side by side. They hadn't been there yesterday. His mother-in-law must have snuck in sometime in the night and placed them there.

He'd made a mistake before, but this time, the moment he saw the two vases, he knew what they were. He didn't know if one of them was the same urn that he'd seen at his mother-in-law's apartment, but the shape was similar. They were made from the same bluish, rounded porcelain.

The other thing, jagi, *that's not* jagi. He could still hear his wife's voice as she teased him, punning on the words for *porcelain* and *sweetheart.* He tried saying it out loud. A hollow shriek gusted out. Back when he and his wife still joked with each other, Oghi had felt embarrassed by the idea of calling her *jagi* as a term of endearment, since the word could also mean *oneself.* Oghi used to muse about having two *jagis*—his *self* and his *beloved.* His wife had two, as well. Though saying it out loud embarrassed him, each time he called her *jagi,* he felt like they were blending together. They liked to say, "What's *jagi*'s problem?" They said it more in reference to themselves as a couple than to one of them alone. They used it, too, when privately chiding themselves.

When Oghi and his wife set out on their trip, they'd started out speaking politely to each other, but their kind words deteriorated the further they got. She seemed to think that the silence filling the car was his fault. At first she only let her unhappiness show on her face, but gradually she began to vent her anger out loud. Oghi lost his anger too—when she suggested splitting up. Oghi firmly refused. Neither of them would benefit from ending their marriage. Oghi knew it, and so did she.

Was that what his wife had wanted? Had she, simply for the purpose of making Oghi angry enough to end it, started telling him what she knew? She told him her plan was to make him lose everything. She said she would make sure it happened. She was more than capable.

But in the end she didn't. Oghi did it to himself. Not because of the car crash, and not because of the irreparable damage he suffered in the crash. He might have been losing everything all along, the whole time that he'd been living his life, possibly since long, long before the crash, starting way back when he first had some vague inkling of what life was. He'd sensed it sometimes. A feeling that, despite how hard he had worked at everything, he was continuously missing something. That was why he sometimes clung all the more tenaciously.

Oghi had wanted to make things clear. He insisted at first that nothing had happened between him and J. He still thought his wife might be bluffing. But it turned out there were things she did know. She fired off the names of several hotels, her face a picture of triumph. She seemed to think that would wring a confession from him. She looked ecstatic that her convictions weren't wrong, that her suspicions were not unfounded. The more excuses he made and the harder he tried to keep looking her in the eye, the more his energy flagged. He was left with no choice but to admit that something had happened, but that it had ended a long time ago. And he swore it would never happen again.

It was depressing to belatedly sort out an old breakup. His affair with J was behind him and he could do nothing about it. Though he didn't deny what he'd done, Oghi felt like he was paying the price for old mistakes.

His wife had mentioned J several times before, but Oghi had never paid it much mind. He saw no point in letting her know each time he ran into J by chance and they grabbed a bite together, or even when they attended the same academic conference outside of the city. Not because it was a secret, but because he knew that his wife had long been suspicious of J. Though he'd never said anything, his wife had put two and two together. Sometimes he inadvertently mentioned J while talking about someone else. Since she wasn't a secret, there was nothing to hide. But whenever that happened, his wife gave him the third degree. Was Oghi hiding something else? There was no end to her suspicions. Each time, Oghi felt like he was covering something up and the conversation would turn to topics that were even harder to discuss with his wife.

She'd become more openly suspicious of J after the barbecue. She even insisted that she saw them together in the
living room that day. J was drunk, and Oghi was helping
her. He didn't know it at the time, but his wife had followed
them into the house to get more alcohol. Unaware that his
wife was standing behind them, he had helped J onto the
sofa. She and Oghi had the closeness that came from having been friends for a long time. He sometimes confused
it for a different emotion, and sometimes got the same
impression from her as well. As J closed her eyes, he tugged
down her jacket, which had crept up to reveal her stomach.
He could have just left the room then, but he stood there
a moment and watched her as she slept. A certain emotion
washed over him, and though he wanted to say something,
he did not. That was all. It had gone no further. He immediately went back out to the yard where everyone else was.

But his wife claimed she'd seen him hug and kiss J.
Oghi laughed. That hadn't happened. When it hit him that
his wife's sudden tyranny, her anger and her mood changes
as she randomly showered Oghi with curses and spat out
hateful things about his colleagues and about J in particular,
all while tearing up their yard, had started from a simple
misunderstanding, he turned despondent. His wife's anger
was not justified. It was sudden, uncontrolled, and violent.

Back then his wife had imagined things. Or maybe
she'd seen the future. What she insisted she had seen didn't
happen the day she said it did. But it did happen later.

"You were mistaken," Oghi had told her repeatedly.

He'd told her everything as he remembered it—what happened the day of the barbecue, what he did, what J did. There was no need to lie. Because nothing *had* happened. But his story felt flimsy. It was obvious to him that he'd done nothing wrong, and yet each time Oghi tried to describe what he remembered in detail or the order in which things had happened, his story changed a little with each retelling. That in and of itself wasn't unusual. But his wife refused to accept that her memory too might have been faulty.

She did not believe Oghi when he told her nothing happened that day. Only when Oghi was worn out from talking did she nod and say, Fine. That meant she didn't so much believe him as that she would be watching him from then on.

Looking back on it, his wife had always been suspicious of him. She thought he was irresponsible, and insisted that he was constantly on the prowl. She would often blindly declare that he had disappointed her, that he had changed. She criticized him for being too caught up in making a name for himself and not taking care of his family. She knit her brows at him, called him a snob. Slapped his hands away, pulled away when he tried to get closer. She had no idea how miserable it made him feel when she did that. Later, after he'd held J in his arms, he inwardly blamed his wife.

Just as she thought, he did start meeting J, but the relationship didn't last long. He let J down as well, and had only himself to blame. He apologized and clung to her, but it was no use. Oghi was heartbroken. He still loved J. There were things he could bear only because of her. At the same time, it surprised him to feel that way. It was refreshing to find that he could suffer from love at his age, and it made him fantasize that he was younger than he really was. The proof was that he had lost love and been hurt by it.

It was difficult and exhausting, but he quickly accepted the fact that life had to go on without her. He'd lost love, and yet the world was not the slightest bit shaken by his loss. The part of his life that had had J in it went away, leaving behind a cavity, a hollow, and still the world was unmoved. Nothing would ever fill in that empty space. But Oghi's world would keep on spinning regardless.

To be human was to be saddled with emptiness, and Oghi made use of this idea in his classes and lectures by saying that that might be the ultimate inner truth. He brought it up while explaining Babylonian maps.

The world's oldest map, the Babylonian Map of the World, had a little circle bored through the center. Scholars explained that the hole had come from using a compass to trace the two outer rings of the map. Oghi was captivated more by that hole than by the geometric shapes engraved in the clay tablet, and had stared at it for a long time in the darkened exhibit room of the British Museum. That dark, narrow hole went as deep as the memory of an age that no one could ever return to. The only way to reach that lost age was through that hole, but the hole itself could never be reached.

Why did his wife think she saw him and J kissing? Why was she so convinced she saw something that didn't actually happen? Maybe she too had felt an enormous cavity open up in the middle of her life. Maybe she'd realized that the life she'd tried so hard to maintain was all for nothing. Maybe in her effort to close that cavity, tormented by a sense of falsehood, she had tended her garden alone, shut herself up in her room, kept on writing in vain despite failing to finish anything she started.

When they were about thirty kilometers from their destination, his wife broke the silence. She said that she'd recently completed a writing project. It had been a long time since she'd talked about writing anything.

"You did? Congratulations! What did you write?" Oghi said without taking his eyes off the road. The number of large vehicles on the road had been slowly increasing.

"It's kind of special. It's an open letter to someone."

"The same letter you were working on last time?" he asked, glancing over at her.

"Maybe it's more like field notes. On how people turn into snobs."

She suddenly laughed. Oghi concentrated on driving. There was no reason to get upset at her. Her goal may have been to make him angry, but his was simply to get them to their destination.

In a small voice, she told him what she'd written. The letter described a man who turned into a snob and used coincidence and trickery to get ahead and detailed how lax his morals were. She added sarcastically that his ongoing inappropriate relationship with a younger colleague was a nice anecdote that highlighted his unique sense of ethics. She said she was planning to send the letter to several different addressees. His department office. His university administration. His academic committees. His colleagues.

Oghi struggled to keep calm. As humiliating as it was, the worst-case scenario his wife was hoping to create would never come to be. Oghi must not have looked shocked enough for her, because she kept going. She told him she'd met with J, which did surprise him. He bumped into J pretty often at school, and she'd never mentioned anything. His wife was surely bluffing, trying to trick him into admitting something.

Or maybe J was still angry with Oghi and wanted to get him in trouble too. He thought he'd apologized sufficiently, but J hadn't accepted his apologies. What'd happened was he had been unable to resist a student's advances. The fling hadn't lasted more than a day. That one day was nothing compared to all of the days he'd spent on earth. But that changed when J found out. It turned into a day he would never be able to forget. While being interrogated by J, he genuinely regretted what he had done. He tried to explain to her that he was just trying to comfort the student when one thing led to another, but J didn't believe him.

Oghi got paranoid. If J really was in collusion with his wife, then there could even have been a third person orchestrating all of it. Was it possible that K had talked them into it? Did K resort to the same tactics that Oghi had used back when he was on the job market? Oghi had known some unsavory things about K, and he'd put those things into a convincing arrangement and presented them to M, and then dropped sly hints to loose-lipped S as well. It was a low move, but it's not like it was unfounded slander. Even if Oghi did use it to his advantage. Sometimes one's own success wasn't enough. Sometimes the failure of someone closer to you was better insurance.

He'd been through so much already, but because of things that should've stayed in the past, because of old history he couldn't do a damn thing about anymore, he had to put up with the third degree from his wife. She laughed at him. Nothing was in the past, she said. Oghi didn't respond to that and declared instead that he refused to get a divorce. He said that to make her angry. And she did get angry. When Oghi mocked her, saying, "You're nothing without me. You can't even earn a living!" she punched him as he drove. She stomped her feet so hard that it echoed through the chassis. She grabbed his arms as he held on to the wheel and shook them.

If she hadn't done that, would they have been okay? If she hadn't told him what she was writing, if she had tried to calmly enjoy their weekend away and work on their relationship as they'd said they would when they first set out on the road, if Oghi had meekly apologized right away when she couldn't resist bringing up J again, if he had not made fun of his wife's incompetence?

Those were the hypotheticals Oghi considered while staring out at the blackness of the asphalt. None of his suppositions were optimistic. He felt certain that even if they moved on from that moment safely, something similar would come up before long and repeat itself over and over without end.

Oghi weakened and felt the cavity inside of him yawn open uncontrollably. He felt like throwing himself into that hole. The large vehicle blocking the view in front of him looked like a hole. It grew difficult to breathe, the pressure in his chest worsened. He was dizzy and on the verge of passing out from fatigue. He possessed a fierce attachment to life, but the impotence of that moment also refused to leave him. His wife wrenched at Oghi's arm as he held the steering wheel. Shocked, he shook her hands off as hard as he could.

They rear-ended the truck in front of them, smashed through the guardrail, and tumbled downhill. The moment he realized what was happening, Oghi relaxed. It was over. He felt free and easy. Though it was unfair to have worked so hard to make a life for himself only to lose it now, the fatigue of having to keep up that lifestyle was worse. Oghi waited to float up out of his body, to rise and put some distance between himself and the face of the earth.

Despite his wishes, Oghi was piledriven into the ground. His body was so heavy, he felt like he'd been buried deep below the earth. In the end, Oghi failed at sending his body aloft, into thin air.

His wife, at last, found success. While Oghi was squashed under the heavy heel of an impenetrable darkness, she grew light as smoke. She floated up and distanced herself from the earth. Perhaps she was even looking down at Oghi.

It was difficult to picture what look she might have had on her face while looking down at him. Had she grabbed his arm in order to steer them into the truck in front of them? Or was she trying to stop Oghi from doing the same? He had no way of knowing. Clueless as to whether his wife had tried to save or assist Oghi as he sped into the truck, Oghi had survived while his wife died.

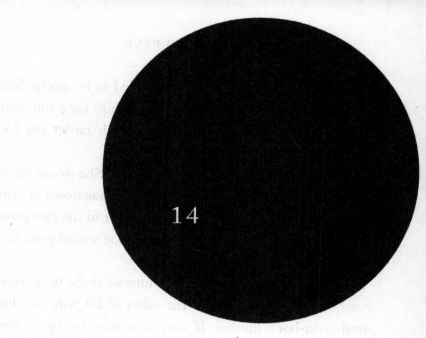

14

GREENERY FILLED THE WINDOW. THE handful of vine stems his mother-in-law had twined around the bars had quickly grown over the entire grating. He saw nothing but green. Now and then a breeze rustled the leaves and he caught a quick glimpse of the garden between them.

He couldn't see much, but he heard noises coming from outside. He guessed from the sounds out there that his mother-in-law had not given up on the garden and was probably still digging the pond. The silence was broken by thuds, by the clanging of metal tools, by the sound of pouring.

How big and deep was the pit?

Not being able to see the garden made it hard to keep track of where his mother-in-law was. She would enter the house without making a sound and go from this room to that before suddenly flinging his door open. Each time she did, Oghi closed his eyes and pretended to be asleep. She would stand at a distance and examine him for a moment before closing the door, only after which he let out his breath.

Sometimes she did it late at night too. She would burst into his room, stand next to his bed and gaze down at him as he pretended to sleep, and then go over to the two urns. After wiping them with a white cloth, she would press her hands together lightly and murmur.

His mother-in-law never told him what the urns were, but he'd assumed they held the ashes of his wife and his mother-in-law's mother. If not, then who on earth was in there? But now he was beginning to think maybe that wasn't the case. Maybe one did hold his wife's ashes, but maybe the other was empty. And waiting for Oghi.

Regardless of whether his eyes were open or closed, his mother-in-law sometimes abruptly asked, "What do you think?" It was better to be prepared when that happened. It meant she was about to do something to him. Usually something he didn't want her to do. His mother-in-law did whatever she wanted with no regard for his reaction.

It had happened the night before as well. His mother-in-law had come in without bothering to turn on the light and walked up to him as he pretended to sleep. She'd said, "What do you think? Your hair's getting a bit long, isn't it?" and held a pair of scissors to his head. She grabbed a rough fistful of Oghi's hair and hacked at it ruthlessly.

Each time he heard the snip-snip of the blades in the dark, his immobile body seemed to cringe. When the snipping sound came close to the rim of his ear, he squeezed his eyes tight in dread.

Now his face itched horribly, as if the snippets of hair were sticking there. His left hand was busy scratching everywhere it could reach. The itch spread until he was going back and forth from one stiff leg to the other. He switched to the back scratcher the caregiver had left behind. As he did so, he realized that his left thigh seemed to register the sharp edge of the scratcher.

Oghi tried flexing. His left leg twitched. He was sure of it. It was very faint, but the muscle contracted and relaxed.

This time he pinched his leg with his left hand. He hadn't felt any pain even when bedsores broke out on his back and bottom. It was only when his mother-in-law made a face and bandaged him up that he realized anything was wrong. But this time he felt it. The pain was very faint, but there was a definite brief, sharp sensation. Even without being looked after by a caregiver, even without the help of a physical therapist, without his doctor's checkups and prescriptions, Oghi's rotting log of a body was gradually coming back to life.

When his mother-in-law came in to clean the urns, he hid his new discovery. He did not tell her that he'd moved his left leg approximately ten centimeters to the side. After wiping the urns, his mother-in-law stared down at him,

179

causing his body to itch all over, but he willed himself not to move. His plan was to not reveal to her that he was getting better.

When he was alone, he diligently practiced moving his legs left and right on the bed. He had not forgotten the exercises from his physical therapy sessions in the hospital. He was careful not to overdo it and break another blood vessel like last time. He could drag his legs along the mattress, but he still couldn't lift them. But it was just a matter of time. Gradually he was able to noticeably wiggle the fingers of his right hand. If the doctor could see him, he would no doubt cheer him on and remind him: *Willpower, not medical power.*

He said nothing, but his mother-in-law picked up on the change in Oghi's expression.

"Did you have a good dream or something?" she asked.

Her voice was hard. It was a bad idea to tell her he was happy. He kept his mouth shut.

"As if anything good could happen to you," she said mockingly as she left the room. "May as well try to dream."

This wasn't a dream. She had no idea, but Oghi felt movement. He felt pain. He felt itchy. He felt alive. He felt it in his body.

If he could get proper treatment in the hospital, his recovery would go much faster. But he didn't know how to get there. He briefly considered whether he should tell his mother-in-law the truth, but he just as quickly changed his mind. She would never help Oghi. He thought about the look on her face when his doctor had said his prognosis was good. If he told her he was getting better, she would only feel more afraid.

The next day, Oghi began refusing to eat. It had been a long time since his mother-in-law had made sure he was fed regularly, but he still turned down her sporadic attempts at feeding him. She got annoyed at him for refusing to open his mouth. He shook his head weakly. With practice, he could have been able to lift a spoon, he could have been able to swallow rice porridge instead of formula, but his mother-in-law would not give up on the liquid food. She didn't want him to get better. She would not take him back to the hospital. It was obvious that only when his body was broken beyond repair, only when there was nothing they could do for him, would she seek the hospital's help.

Whenever his mother-in-law looked at him, Oghi closed his eyes and acted weak. At first he had to force himself, but after a few days he really wasn't feeling well. She watched him more and more frequently. Oghi moaned and dripped with sweat. His moans of pain came out on their own, without his having to dress them up.

Once he even caught himself murmuring *Tasukete kuda-sai* along with his mother-in-law. He heard the words come out clearly. He had no idea how long it had been since he'd heard his own raspy voice or anything decipherable coming out of him. His mother-in-law must have been just as surprised, but she tried to pretend otherwise. Oghi frowned to disguise the sounds coming out of his mouth.

His mother-in-law stopped looking after him alto-gether. She did nothing. Since he refused to eat, she stopped bringing him any food at all and only provided him with a bare minimum of drinking water. Before long Oghi was in a critical state. The fever that wracked his body and the humidity in the room made him feel like a weight was pressing down on his chest. It became difficult to breathe.

The person his mother-in-law reluctantly called to check up on Oghi was the physical therapist. Oghi watched through a fever dream as they came into his room, talking noisily.

"He's in pretty bad shape," the therapist said the second he saw Oghi.

"Bad enough to have to go to the hospital?"

The therapist sounded surprised by the question.

"You haven't taken him to the hospital? He absolutely must go. His fever is very high, and those bedsores are really bad. At this rate. . ."

The therapist became aware that Oghi was listening and caught himself.

"I'll take care of him today, but now is not the time for therapy. He needs to be in the hospital. He's in critical condition."

Oghi's mother-in-law left the room looking haggard. Oghi mustered up what strength he could to speak to the therapist. His voice must not have been audible, because the therapist came closer to him.

I can move my legs.

The therapist couldn't understand him. Oghi had clearly heard his own words. Why couldn't the therapist? Oghi mustered his strength again and forced the words out. The therapist stared at him for a moment and chuckled.

"Yes, you're right. It has been a long time. I bet you're happy to see me. I'm telling you, I should have been coming to see you this whole time. I assumed you were busy getting treatment at the hospital. You kept going on about the hospital, the hospital, and never even went. And now look at the shape you're in."

Oghi repeated himself again. This time, he mouthed the word, spelling it out one letter at a time, as big as he could.

"L-E-G. Leg?"

The therapist looked at Oghi's legs. Oghi flexed. His leg inched over to the side. He wanted to show the therapist what he had accomplished on his own while he was gone. It was still impossible to lift his leg, but he could push it toward the edge of the mattress.

"You want me to start with your legs?"

Oghi was disappointed that he still hadn't caught on. He asked for paper and slowly wrote the words: *LEG MOVED.* The therapist looked at him in surprise. Then he stared at Oghi's leg for a long time. Oghi moved it once more for him. He could not have missed it this time.

"Uh, I'm not sure how to tell you this. Please don't be disappointed. This is actually quite common for people in your condition."

The therapist looked at him sympathetically and gave his thin leg a gentle pat.

"It can sometimes feel like a paralyzed limb is moving. Like you're experiencing now. But it doesn't actually move at all. Some doctors refer to it as 'rejection of paralysis syndrome.' It's a type of hallucination. But this doesn't mean you should lose heart. It may be a hallucination, but it's also a reflection of how strong your will is. The will to walk, the will to move on your own. That's important for people like you. Without that, it's easy to give up."

Rejection of paralysis. Oghi found this strange new term appalling. He knew his own body. It had taken a long time to reach its current shape, but it had been with him since birth. His body was his closest ally, his constant companion. It wasn't like his spirit or his heart, which never did what he wanted them to, which acted of their own accord, with no respect to him.

Oghi was acutely aware of his body's minor aches and itches, the tautness of his skin, the sagging. He easily recognized hunger and fullness, even phantom symptoms of diabetes. Of course there were times when he wasn't quite so certain. Times when he couldn't quite identify which part of him ached. He'd once had a boil for a long time without knowing it. When the caregiver had pressed against him, his body had disobeyed him, and when tempted by a girl much too young for him, he'd gotten aroused. But for the most part it had always moved in accordance with his will.

"Let's give this another try. Move your left leg."

Oghi did as he was told. It was difficult, but he wanted the therapist to believe him.

"And now the right leg."

When he looked at the therapist's face, he lost hope. The therapist gave Oghi no encouragement.

Next the therapist instructed him to tell him which leg he was touching. Oghi said it was the right leg and knew from looking at him that he was wrong. He seemed to answer the next one correctly, but the therapist looked no more convinced.

After a long pause, the therapist told him that his legs had changed. He didn't mean that Oghi could now move them, he meant they were dangerously atrophied. Though it was common for patients' bodies to become imbalanced, in Oghi's case, it was progressing at an exceptionally rapid pace. He used up the remaining appointment time trying to convince Oghi that it would be difficult to recover mobility in his legs and that they couldn't be optimistic.

On his way out of the house, the therapist appeared to stop and discuss the problem at length with Oghi's mother-in-law. Naturally, not long after he'd gone through the front gate, she came to Oghi's room.

"Why are you still lying there?" she said, holding her hand out to him. "Come take a walk in the garden with me."

It wasn't too dark for Oghi to make out his mother-in-law's wide grin.

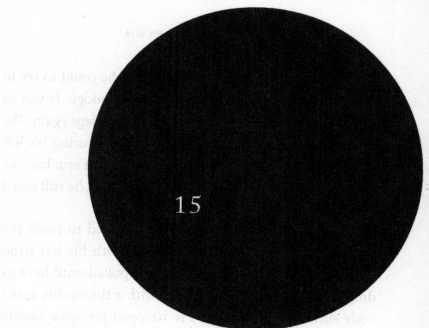

15

His mother-in-law rarely went out, but he knew she couldn't stay in the house forever. Oghi kept exercising his arms, including the right arm that had just recently begun to recover sensation.

The physical therapist had told him he was hallucinating. His mother-in-law had laughed at him. But his right arm *was* getting better. He could move whichever finger he wanted, and he could pinch his left arm with his right hand. No one knew more precisely than Oghi that his body was on the mend. He was determined to prove it to himself. If he could make it out of the house, he would find help and get to a doctor.

Oghi concentrated on the sounds outside. He heard his mother-in-law walk out the front gate and shut it behind her. A moment passed, and the gate did not reopen. He rushed into action. He grabbed the edge of the mattress with his left hand and pulled as hard as he could to try to drag his body over. His body would not budge. It was as stiff and heavy as a fallen tree. He flexed his legs again. The veins popped out on his arms. He'd been favoring his left arm for so long that the difference in his right arm became obvious. Though he could move the right arm, he still relied heavily on the left.

After a great deal of sweat, he managed to reach the edge of the bed. He grabbed the rail with his left hand and the headboard with his right and pulled until his legs dropped to the floor. They landed with a thump, his upper body slithering after them. He wrapped his arms around his head as he fell. Even after the rest of him hit the floor, he felt no pain in his lower half. His legs were useless. Oghi finally believed what the physical therapist had been trying to tell him.

Using only his arms, he dragged himself across the floor. The first crisis came in front of the tightly shut bedroom door. He lifted both arms but to no avail. Oghi crawled back and grabbed the back scratcher that had fallen off of the bed with him. He reached up with his left arm and hooked the scratcher over the horizontal doorknob. It slipped. It wasn't going to work. His whole body was drenched with sweat. The cold floor did nothing to mitigate his fever. He hooked the back scratcher over the doorknob again and tugged, over and over. The light in the room had dimmed by the time he was able to get the knob open.

The living room was even darker than his bedroom. Heavy curtains covered the wide front window. Once his eyes had adjusted to the darkness, he realized that the living room was completely changed. It didn't look like anyone lived there. As if everyone had moved out long ago.

Their sofa, upholstered in a Danish designer fabric, that his wife had so carefully chosen and waited three whole months to have delivered, was gone. In its place was a large leather couch. It looked like it had come from his mother-in-law's apartment. But more surprising than the couch were the piles of household goods stacked every which way in the center of the living room. There was no order to any of it, as if it hadn't been placed there for organizing but rather had been tossed together prior to being thrown out. Many of the items were from Oghi's study. The green, retro-style lamp that had illuminated Oghi's desk late at night was shoved upside-down into a big cardboard box, and the plaque of appreciation from the mapmakers association was tossed in there as well.

Oghi dragged himself to the front door. He had no idea when his mother-in-law was coming back or how much longer his strength would hold out, but he had to keep going. Opening the front door would be easier than opening his bedroom door. All he had to do was push the green button at the bottom of the digital door lock.

He tried pressing it with the other end of the back scratcher, but it wasn't heavy enough. He knocked over the umbrella stand next to the front door and selected a long umbrella, then tried to use the tip to press the unlock button on the door. The strength in his hand gave out, and the umbrella fell, smacking him on the head and shoulders. He didn't know what else to do and just kept tapping the digital lock with the tip of the umbrella. By the time he got the door open, the cold tile beneath him had turned hot.

Oghi sucked in the cold, fresh air. It was the exact opposite of the stuffy, musty air that filled the house. The air outside smelled and felt so good that he felt like crying.

The garden looked like a vacant lot. Other than the tight row of trees along the low iron fence next to the front gate, there was not a single growing, sprouting, blooming, living thing. The shrubs had all been uprooted and stacked to one side like firewood. There were circles of darkness all over the place. Each one was a small pit. They didn't look like they'd been dug in order to plant something new but were the holes left behind from yanking living plants out of the earth by their roots.

In the middle of the garden, slightly diagonal and to the right of where Oghi lay, the darkness pooled, slick-black and enormous. It was the part of the yard that Oghi could not see from his room. The pool of darkness must have been the huge pit that everyone had talked about.

Soft, loose dirt was piled up around the sides. He assumed that after digging the hole his mother-in-law had lined the bottom with a tarp, so the rain or dew could pool there. Once it filled up enough, she would probably use the loose soil for planting and release carp into the water. Perhaps once Oghi was gone, those carp would be the only living thing at the house along with her. She would raise living creatures, just as she'd said she would.

But on second thought, maybe his mother-in-law wasn't raising carp in order to see something live. Maybe she wanted them so she could watch them die. Even carp in a pond will die eventually. And when they do, their mouths gape and they roll and float to the surface, their bodies as stiff and unmoving as Oghi's.

The gray paving stones that he and his wife had spent so much time discussing and had such a hard time selecting scratched mercilessly at his body. A sour odor, unlike anything he'd smelled before, wafted off of him. It might have been the smell of blood. Blood flowed from a deep scrape on his left arm. But he kept going. Other than his arms, he felt no pain anywhere else. He was, for once, grateful to his heavy, stone-like body. It enabled him to endure this.

Oghi paused on the paving stones and looked up at the iron gate. It didn't look like he would be able to open it using an umbrella or a back scratcher. After trying and failing, he decided it would be better to crawl to the fence and get help from a neighbor. Fortunately, his neighbors often went for walks on nights like these, when a fresh breeze was blowing. There were enough people around that, if he had to, he could just stick his hand through the fence and someone would help him.

Slowly, slowly, he made his way across the garden. Whenever yellow headlights came toward the house, he stopped, and when they passed, he leaned into his arms again. Several times, headlights approached and scanned over his body like a searchlight before moving on. Once more, he waited for a pair of lights to pass, but this time they stayed in one spot and did not move. All he could do was make himself as flat as possible and hope that the dark would hide him.

The gate opened with a soft sound. Slowly his mother-in-law entered. He thought it was over, but there was still a chance. She hadn't seen him. She walked along the paving stones and into the house. The darkness helped, along with the fact that she wouldn't be expecting to see him in the garden.

He had to go a little further. He leaned into his arms again. When the dirt touched his scraped-up arms, they stung more than he could bear and ached as if tiny pebbles were digging into his torn skin. He was lucky to have made it out of the house, but now he realized he was risking losing both arms as well. Nevertheless, he kept pulling himself along as hard as he could.

His mother-in-law rushed back out. It hadn't taken her long to discover his door sitting open. He stared at her as she stood stock-still before the front door. Her long shadow forked in front of her. He lay still and did not move. The shadow of his mother-in-law's body, made bigger by the darkness, stepped down onto the paving stones.

He knew she wasn't strong enough to drag him. Just as no one had helped him to get out of the house, no one was going to help her to get him back in. He could choose whether to go back, or to keep crawling along the fence until he found help. He didn't have to ponder it long. Ignoring his mother-in-law as she slowly walked toward him where he lay flat in the garden, Oghi chose to keep going.

There was one thing Oghi hadn't considered. Though his mother-in-law did not have the strength to pick him up, she did have enough strength to get in his way.

She blocked his path. She did it with her two thick, sturdy legs, planting them just out of reach of his arms. He tried in vain to grab her legs and then had no choice but to change direction to avoid those trunk-like limbs. Too late he realized that she was steering him exactly where she wanted him to go.

Oghi stopped not on flat land but at the low ridge of loose dirt. On the other side was an enormous pool of darkness. The darkness gave off a chill. His body shook. The dirt lining the round sides of the hole felt different from the type of dirt he'd spent his life walking on. It was subsoil, not topsoil. The particles were very fine. It was the same soil he had touched long ago, when he'd helped his wife to till the yard.

Oghi turned to avoid the pit, but he couldn't avoid his mother-in-law's stubbornly planted legs. Each time he went around her, he ended up closer to the soft soil.

His mother-in-law brought her foot up threateningly. Fearful that she was about to stomp on his spine, he turned. The loosely piled dirt collapsed beneath him, and his body tipped downward. He tried to stop himself from falling but only pressed down harder on the loose, shifting dirt. He lost his balance and tumbled helplessly.

Pain. He felt pain. It was completely different from what he'd felt when he thought his legs were moving. He couldn't tell if the pain was a sign of survival or the agony that came with dying. It made him happy, even if he did have no way out now. It had been a long time since he'd felt even this kind of pain. His arms, of course, but also his lower back and his bony legs were sending him pain messages. It was identical to the pain he'd felt when the car carrying him and his wife tumbled down the hill.

He was certain it wouldn't be long now before he saw his wife again. Once the overwhelming pain passed, he would at last float up out of his body. He would ascend into the air and look down at himself sprawled miserably at the bottom of the pit. It surprised him that it had been less than a year since his wife had looked down on him like that. Those intervening months had felt so very, very long.

The person looking down on Oghi now was not his wife. It was his mother-in-law. Her arms were crossed, and she stood as still as a statue as she stared down at him trapped at the bottom. The distance was immense. He could tell how far away he was from the fact that her face looked just like his wife's.

The pain continued and worsened each time he touched some part of himself. But as he did so, he realized he could no longer feel the dirt and pebbles beneath him. His body stiffened, and his breath grew light. The pain passed. After a moment, it vanished completely and he felt instantly at peace.

While looking up at the dark sky from the bottom of the hole, he remembered that he'd been here before. Not here, as in the bottom of a pit, but here in the yard, sitting in this same spot at the picnic table, talking to his wife. A day when they'd shared a light dinner and gone for a walk in the neighborhood. An evening spent looking for the place where a cat had once startled them both by bolting out from under a parked car, so they could set some food out and wait at a distance to see if the cat would reappear. A day when they had watched the cat appear from out of nowhere, eat all the food, and then crawl back under the car, after which they returned home and talked for a long time about random, silly things. An evening when they ended their long day by reading together outside until they were both drowsy. A night spent talking about the book before lying down on freshly laundered sheets and drifting into sleep. A day when simple, leisurely tasks repeated themselves like the squares on a *baduk* board. The kind of perfectly peaceful day found in any given life. One day from among many days entirely different from now.

His wife had looked up from her book and her face had gone suddenly slack. Oghi knew all of his wife's expressions, and this one was no different.

"Sleepy? Shall we turn in?"

"No."

"Then what is it?"

"I'm sad. . ."

"Huh?"

His wife slowly recited the part she'd just read in her book. It was the story of a man who narrowly escapes death. One day as he's walking past a construction site, a beam falls and lands right in front of him. Though he isn't injured, he realizes how close he has come to dying and comes up with an idea.

"Why is that sad? That's lucky."

"He disappears. He leaves everything behind, even his savings, and takes off without bothering to quit his job or cancel any of his appointments. He doesn't leave any clues for his friends or family or colleagues either, but just vanishes completely. Just like that. His wife hires a detective to look for him. She worries that he could be hurt or in a coma somewhere or wandering around with amnesia, not knowing who his family is. That's the only way she can accept his disappearance. After a while, the detective tracks him down. He's alive and safe and living in another city where he has changed his name and found a new job. With his new family."

"I guess his wife wasn't too happy about that."

"I don't think it's that. I think it's what she learns from it."

"What?"

Instead of answering, she'd stared at him.

196

Oghi quickly asked, "That he can have a good life some-where else without her?"

That time as well she simply stared at him. Oghi had grown impatient and tried a different tack.

"So then what happens?"

"That's the end."

"He doesn't go back to his family?"

"It says they get a divorce."

"That's pretty mean. Do they at least end up happy?"

She'd started crying. At first he thought she was just tearing up a little, but soon she was sobbing loudly. Why? Because of a man lucky enough to survive a freak accident? Because of a man who leaves one day? Because of a man who makes a new life for himself that's hardly any different from his old life? Was that why she was crying?

Oghi looked at his crying wife and laughed. How was that a sad story? What a thing to cry over. Had his wife always been this emotional? It made no sense to him, but he was amused by her sentimentality and wanted to make her feel better. We'll always be together, he told her, no matter what happens, I won't cross over into the great beyond without you. It wasn't until much later that he realized how much better it would've been if he'd let her find her own way out of this grief, slowly, without any empty promises or hasty conclusions. Oghi had quietly held his wife, who seemed to be experiencing some future grief that had not yet taken place, and watched as her tears slowed and then stopped.

The fact that he was now lying at the bottom of a deep, dark hole did not mean that Oghi finally understood his wife's grief. But it did make him realize how completely he had failed at comforting her. His wife's tears had stopped not because she was no longer sad, but because the time had come to stop crying.

And at last, Oghi cried. Not because of his wife. But because his time for crying had come.